PRAISE FOR **THE TEMPLETON TWINS HAVE AN IDEA:**

A Parents' Choice Approved Award Winner
A Kids' Indie Next Pick

★ "A page-turning and funny tale."
—Shelf Awareness for Readers, starred review

"An entertaining start to a new series."
—*School Library Journal*

"Readers . . . will welcome this and the duo's
future exploits." —*Booklist*

"The scene-hogging narrator steals the show in this
clever series opener." —*Kirkus Reviews*

"Illustrations . . . play up the story's humor
as well as highlighting the twins' ingenuity."
—*The Horn Book*

# THE TEMPLETON TWINS

## TWINS

### HAVE AN IDEA

## TO BARBARA DAVILMAN. —ELLIS WEINER
## TO PAXTON AND CHARLIE HOLMES. —JEREMY HOLMES

First paperback edition published in 2013 by Chronicle Books LLC.
Originally published in hardcover in 2012 by Chronicle Books LLC.

ISBN 978-1-4521-2704-0

The Library of Congress has cataloged the original edition as follows:
Library of Congress Cataloging-in-Publication Data

Weiner, Ellis.
The Templeton twins have an idea / by Ellis Weiner ; illustrations by Jeremy Holmes.
p. cm. — (The Templeton twins)
Summary: Abigail and John, the Templeton twins, and their dog Cassie,
foil a pair of inept kidnappers intent on stealing one of their father's newest inventions.
ISBN 978-0-8118-6679-8 (alk. paper)
1. Twins—Juvenile fiction. 2. Inventors—Juvenile fiction. 3. Kidnapping—
Juvenile fiction. [1. Twins—Fiction. 2. Inventors—Fiction.
3. Kidnapping—Fiction. 4. Humorous stories.] I. Holmes, Jeremy, ill. II. Title.

PZ7.W436359Tem 2012
813.54—dc23

2011049975

Manufactured in China.

MIX
Paper from
responsible sources
FSC
www.fsc.org    FSC® C101537

Book design by Sara Gillingham Studio.
Typeset in Parcel, Chronicle Text, and Chevin.
The illustrations in this book were rendered digitally.

10 9 8 7 6 5 4 3 2 1

Chronicle Books LLC
680 Second Street
San Francisco, CA 94107

Chronicle Books—we see things differently. Become part of our community at www.chroniclekids.com.

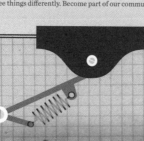

# THE TEMPLETON TWINS

## TWINS

### HAVE AN IDEA

WRITTEN BY
**ELLIS WEINER**

ILLUSTRATED BY
**JEREMY HOLMES**

BOOK 1

chronicle books · san francisco

PROLOGUE:
THE BEGINNING

*The*

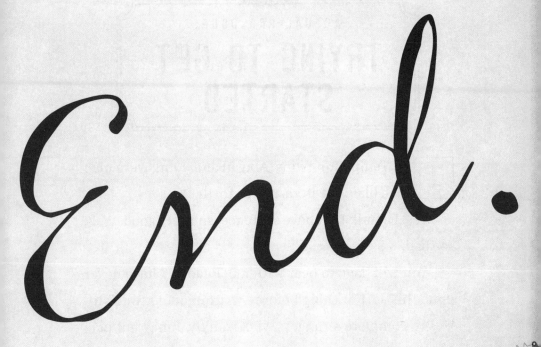

End.

QUESTIONS FOR REVIEW.

1. Did you enjoy the Prologue?

2. Do you think it makes the slightest bit of difference to me whether you did or not?

T he Templeton twins, Abigail and John, were blah blah blah, et cetera, and so forth.

Yes, I admit, the above sentence isn't very good. Well, too bad.

You will have to bear with me, Reader. I have never done this sort of thing before—written books, told stories to complete strangers who, frankly, I may not particularly like. Yes, I am referring to you. Would I like you if I met you? I'm not so sure I would.

Of course, you can say, "Well, maybe I wouldn't like *you* if I met you, Narrator." While that isn't likely, it is indeed a *possibility*. And yet when I contemplate such an occasion, I cannot help but ask myself, *Do I want the Reader to like me? Do I care?*

I think we can all agree that I don't care. Believe me, I am not writing these words because I want to. I am writing them because I am compelled to. That is why I wrote *The End* in the Prologue. I had hoped you would read that and be fooled into thinking you had read an entire book, which I would then not actually have to write.

I had hoped you would look up and say to your parent or guardian or sibling or bodyguard, "My, that was a short book. I'm not sure anything actually happened in it, but it says, 'The End,' so something must have."

However, I can see by the fact that you are reading this now that I was wrong. I was unable to fool you. You must be smarter than I thought. Very well. If you are so terribly, terribly smart, why don't *you* write this book? Just fill it in right here:

_____

_____

_____

I see you have failed to fill it in. It's not as easy as it looks, is it? Fine. **LET'S MOVE ON.**

# ONE DAY, TWELVE YEARS EARLIER—

**HOLD IT,** you may be thinking. "'Earlier' than what? Nothing has happened yet, so how can anything be 'earlier' than nothing?"

In reply, I can say only that it seemed like a good idea to write, "One day, twelve years earlier," but now I am having Second Thoughts. I shall try writing the Prologue again.

But wait. First, let us all agree on what a "Prologue" is. A Prologue is the part of the story that happens before the events of the main story itself. ("Pro-" means "before," and "-logue" means . . . whatever it means. Look it up. Why do I have to do everything?) The purpose of the Prologue is to establish something important that will have consequences later.

There. We all agree on what a Prologue is. That is, I have told you what it is, and you agree with me. Now, at last, finally, here, is the actual Prologue.

# GETTING STARTED *AGAIN*

O ne day, twelve years earlier, Professor Elton Templeton was in his office at Elysian University, talking with a student. Normally the Professor enjoyed meeting with students in his office, but today he was distracted by the fact that his wife was about to give birth to their first baby.

However, he had been told that the baby would not be ready to be born for some time, so he had decided to conduct his usual office hours. He had met with all the students who wished to speak with him except this one.

This young man, who was quite good-looking, had come to the Professor's office to protest the grade the Professor had given him in a course entitled "Introduction to Systems Dynamics." Do you know what that means? Of course you don't. And yet I do .

Fortunately for both you and me, what it means is irrelevant to our story. For now, just bear in mind that the Professor was a renowned engineer and inventor, and so he taught courses in things like systems and dynamics.

The grade the Professor had given this student was an F, which is the worst grade you can possibly get. The Professor had never given anyone an F before (and, in case you are interested, he never would again). He didn't like giving anyone an F, and he didn't like arguing over grades. He was uncomfortable with the entire discussion.

But, as he explained, the good-looking student had left him no choice.

"Look here," the Professor said. "You left me no choice. You cheated on all your exams."

This made the student even more upset. "But I came to all your lectures!"

"Yes, but you slept through them," the Professor said. "And you handed in reports that were proven to have been written by someone else."

The door to the Professor's office opened. Standing there was the secretary of the engineering department. She was very excited.

"Professor!" she said breathlessly. "The hospital called. The babies are coming!"

"Oh, my goodness," the Professor said. As he got up from his desk, he said to the young man, "Now you will have to excuse me; the babies are coming. . . ."

"But we're not finished!" the young man said. "You have to give me at least a C or I'll flunk out of college!"

"I cannot give you a C," the Professor said, hastily stuffing papers into his briefcase and grabbing his hat.

"You can't go!" the young man said. "You have to listen to me!"

"Our meeting is concluded," the Professor said. "The babies are coming, and I must be at the hospital."

The Professor was about to hurry out of the building when something occurred to him. He stopped at the secretary's desk.

**DID YOU SAY 'BABIES'?** he asked.

She had. As Professor Elton Templeton discovered upon arriving at the hospital, his wife had had *two* babies, which, as you may know, is twice as many as one. Somehow, when the doctors had given Professor Templeton's wife her checkups, they had not seen that there were two babies, one boy and one girl.

Professor Templeton was amazed and delighted by this news. After visiting his wife to make sure she was all right (she was), he went to the nursery, which is a special room in the hospital where newly born babies sleep during the time they are not with their mothers.

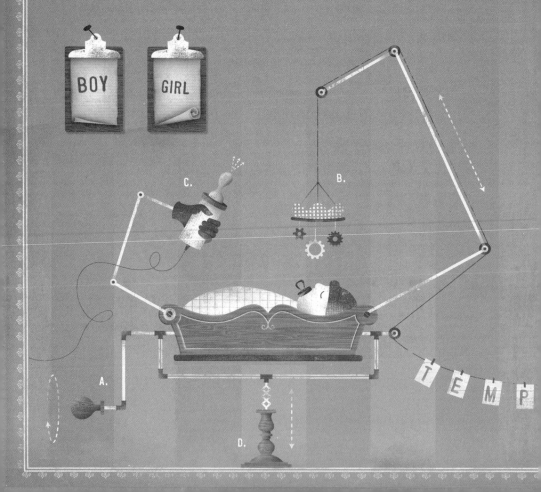

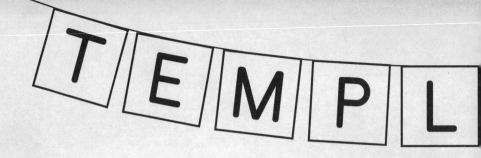

The Professor found a spot among the other adults looking through the big glass window at the various sleeping babies. Each one slept in a little shallow bed hung with a card showing the mother's last name. A long card reading TEMPLETON stretched across two beds in which two babies slept side by side. One wore a blue cap and the other wore a pink cap.

(As you may be aware, when it comes to babies it is not obvious who is a boy and who is a girl. For this reason, some people make sure that boy babies wear blue clothes and girl babies wear pink clothes, to signal who is what. If the color-coded clothes make the babies look fabulous, all the better.)

The Professor did what all new parents do: He tapped on the window and made silly little cooing noises in an effort to get the attention of his just-born, deeply sleeping babies. The Professor was wearing his customary clothes, which included a pair of baggy white pants and

# E T O N

a billowy white shirt. He looked as though he worked for the hospital. Maybe that was why, when a man standing next to him saw the Professor tapping on the window, he became curious and asked, "Who are they?"

"They?" the Professor replied.

**WHY, THEY ARE THE TEMPLETON TWINS.**

## QUESTIONS FOR REVIEW

1. The author has succeeded in writing an actual Prologue. Aren't you proud of him?

2. What do you mean, "no"?

3. Explain, in fifty words or less, why you believe the story will actually get started, and why it will be wonderful.

CHAPTER 1

# THE STORY ACTUALLY *DOES* GET STARTED

A.

B.

START

C.

**T**he Templeton twins, Abigail and John, were twelve years old when their mother died. The woman had been quite ill for some time, and her death was not unexpected. Still, it was a very sad event for the twins, and for their father, Professor Elton Templeton.

## THERE. WE HAVE BEGUN.

### QUESTIONS FOR REVIEW

1. What were the names of Abigail and John, the Templeton twins?

2. Bonus Question: There is no Bonus Question. Proceed to Question 3.

3. Isn't it a splendid thing that we have begun? (Hint: No. It isn't. It means I must write some more. **LET'S MOVE ON.)**

# CHAPTER 2

# YOU MAY STOP COMPLAINING, BECAUSE WE HAVE BEGUN

START

A.

B.

C.

The Templeton twins' mother, as we have discussed *as recently as one page ago,* died when the twins were twelve years old.

Now, if I were you, I would not want to read about how sad the twins and their father were. In fact, if I were me—which, I can assure you, I am—I would not want to read about it, either. And I certainly would not want to have to write about it.

But I *am* going to write about it. Why? Because, as I believe I have already explained, I have to. I am being forced to tell the story of the Templeton twins. Why am I being forced, and who is forcing me? Well, perhaps I will tell you later. Or I may decide not to tell you at all. For now, that doesn't matter.

What matters is that I'm telling you their story, and the only proper way to tell the story of the Templeton twins is to talk about their hobbies and, a little later, their dog. Their hobbies, as you will see, will turn out to be very important to what the twins did and why they did it. And their dog, as will be plain to every eye, was completely ridiculous.

How is this possible? How can hobbies be so important? How can a dog be ridiculous?

Please, kindly stop asking me all these questions. You do your job, which is reading, and I'll do mine, which is narrating. You are the Reader. I am the Narrator. Do we understand each other?

However, I just realized that the one asking the questions is really me. I am therefore in the position of having to ask myself to stop asking questions. Will I do so? Yes, I will. I will what? Ask myself to stop, or stop asking?

All right, I hope you are satisfied. I am now completely confused. I would say, "Let's move on," but I don't even know where we are. **LET'S START OVER.**

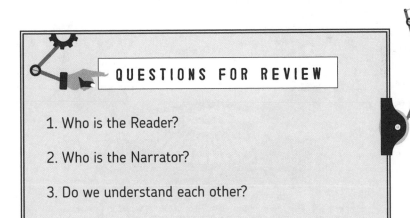

**QUESTIONS FOR REVIEW**

1. Who is the Reader?

2. Who is the Narrator?

3. Do we understand each other?

# THE STORY,
## IN SPITE OF EVERYTHING,
# AT LONG LAST, REALLY
# DOES GET STARTED

T|he Templeton twins **BLAH BLAH, VERY SAD, ET CETERA.** At first friends and neighbors and students came to their home to cook meals, to help out, and to offer comfort. And the Templetons were very grateful.

Then some time passed, because it always does. And while the Professor told his friends that he no longer needed their help, he remained very sad. He could not bring himself to resume teaching or to get back to work on his inventions. He spent most of his time in his study at home, reading and sighing.

Abigail and John, meanwhile, went back to school. They caught up with the material they had missed, and took a test for which they had been absent (they each did pretty well on it). They began to see friends again and to do the things that twelve-year-olds do.

They also went back to pursuing their hobbies, which we will discuss in magnificent detail very shortly.

During this period, it was quite common for the twins to not see their father at all from the time they arrived home from school until dinner. He remained in his study, while they were to be found either in the kitchen, making snacks, or in their rooms.

And so it was . . .

"And so it was." Isn't that wonderful? This is something we normally don't say in ordinary conversation but which I, as a Narrator, am allowed to say without seeming "strange" or "odd" or "weird."

*And so it was* that, after school one day, having enjoyed a snack of frozen waffles and honey, and having washed the dishes, the twins headed up to their rooms. While chatting *en route* (which means "on the way"), they decided to devise a Plan to convince their father to get them something they had wanted for a long time.

I refer, of course, to a dog.

The Templeton twins had been asking their parents for a dog for at least a year. Now, the drama of children asking for a dog is as old as the human (and dog) race. I would not be surprised to learn that Cain and Abel, who, as you may know, were the children of Adam and Eve, asked their parents for a dog, too.

And I expect Adam said, "When you're older," and Cain said, "It's not fair!" and Abel said, "You won't have to walk it or feed it or anything! We'll do all that!" Then, I'm sure, Eve said, "We'll think about it," and Cain said,

"That means no!" and Adam said, "You do not talk to your mother that way," and Cain said, "I'm sorry. But we really want a dog!" and Eve said, "We'll see," and Abel said, "PLEEEEEEASE?" and Adam said, "Drop it. We'll talk about it later," and so on—all of it in Aramaic or Hebrew or whatever it was they spoke in biblical times. (This scene, of Cain and Abel asking Adam and Eve for a dog, is not in the Bible, no. But that doesn't mean it didn't happen.)

Professor Templeton and his wife had kept putting off the matter by saying, "Yes, but not now. When you're older." This, as every child knows, is an outrageous and insulting "reason" for not doing something, and the twins were as indignant and offended as you would expect. Then, of course, came the family's tragedy, and no one mentioned the subject for some time.

Lately, though, the twins had begun to feel that a more normal life was returning to the household. So after the waffles they went to Abigail's room to discuss the matter. They discovered, as they usually did, that they agreed with each other completely. They still wanted a dog.

Abigail was sitting on her bed, wearing blue jeans and a gray T-shirt. She had brown eyes and long, dark hair that she usually wore in a ponytail. She looked much like, but not *exactly* like, her brother.

"I was thinking," she said. "If we just ask Papa the way we usually do, it'll be kind of tedious and grim."

Now, if I were you, I would immediately think, "Just a moment, Narrator. Do you seriously expect me to believe that a twelve-year-old child would use the words 'tedious' and 'grim' in private conversation with her brother? Wouldn't she be much more likely to say something along the lines of 'But, like, John? If we ask Dad the same old way, won't it be, like, boring and sad and stuff?'"

Normally you would be right to ask that. But Abigail Templeton was—well, I won't say she was a genius with words, but I will say that she was very, very smart when it came to words. At the age of twelve, you or I might not use the words "tedious" or "grim," but Abigail did.

John was seated cross-legged on the floor. He, too, had brown eyes and dark hair, although his hair was short. He wore gray jeans and a dark blue T-shirt. John, of course, was accustomed to hearing his sister use interesting and expressive words. When she made her comment, all he said was, "Really? Why?"

"It'll be tedious because it will remind him of all the times we've asked before. And it will be grim because it will remind him of Mama."

John nodded. Then he said, "Hmm. Yeah. Right. Wow. Okay."

Do you see—as I'm sure you do, and as I'm sure *I* do—the difference in the way the twins spoke? "Tedious and grim" versus "Yeah. Right." They were twins, these Templeton twins, but they weren't alike in every way. You will see more of this sort of thing as we proceed.

Abigail said, "We need an exciting and a *commanding* way to ask him. We need a way that will really get his attention."

John agreed, and so the twins discussed various exciting and commanding ways of asking their father for a dog. John suggested writing a song about it. Abigail suggested sending their father a telegram. John suggested writing a note in "invisible ink" (lemon juice), which they would then "miraculously" make visible.

None of these ideas seemed quite right. Both twins were silent in thought. Then John had an idea.

"We can't ask him in a way that *we* think is excellent. It has to be a way that *he'll* think is excellent," he said. "We need some kind of *device.*"

John said "device" in a manner that was just like the way the Professor said it when referring to his inventions. It was a kind of Templeton family code word or private joke. Professor Templeton would come up from his basement workshop, or arrive home from the university, looking preoccupied and vexed. If the twins asked what was bothering him, he would say, "I'm having trouble with the *device,*" or "The *device* isn't quite right yet," or even "I have come to believe that the reason the device does not yet work is that it needs a certain kind of *device.*"

Abigail now said, "Yes! Great! *And* we shouldn't just ask for a dog in general. We should ask for a specific dog. Because then he'll know we've really thought about it."

In fact, they had thought about it, and they did have a specific dog in mind. And so they conceived and refined their Plan.

The next day, when the twins came home from school, they flew into action. Note here that I do not mean that they lifted off the ground and started zooming around the house. I mean they got very busy.

Abigail dug out of her desk drawer an old magazine with a photograph of the dog they both wanted. The twins had been carefully storing it for a year. She cut out the photo and pasted it onto a piece of cardboard.

John, meanwhile, spent some time walking between the kitchen and the dining room with his head tilted back, looking up at the ceiling.

If Abigail was quite clever when it came to words (which she was), John was extremely clever when it came to doing things, to devising plans and putting them into action. His favorite thing to say was **"LET'S DO IT AND VIEW IT!"** He thought he had heard someone say this on a pay phone in the lobby of a movie theater once, and John decided it was a good, brisk way of saying, "Let's try this idea out and then examine it and see if it works."

(Actually, what the person on the phone had said was "Let's do it and then review it," but John misheard his snappier version. It's just as well, don't you think? Don't you believe, as I do, that things should be as snappy as possible? Oh, please. Yes, you do.)

John said it about everything, no matter how important or silly. Would peanut butter be good on pizza? "Let's do it and view it!" If your shoes had no laces, how far could you run before they came off? "Let's do it and view it!" On a hot summer's day, could you really fry an egg on the sidewalk? "Let's . . ." et cetera.

Before you could do and view anything, though, you first had to "figure out what's what." This meant that, in addition to figuring out *what* you wanted to accomplish, you also had

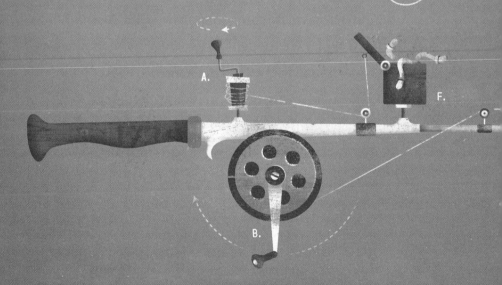

to figure out
*how* to accomplish
it. That's what John did
now as he surveyed the ceiling
in the dining room and the kitchen.

D.

When he had successfully figured out
what was what, he went to the garage and got a
fishing rod that the family sometimes took on trips to the
lake. He made sure a hook was attached to the end of its
line, got a small sinker out of the box of fishing supplies,
and tied that to the end of the line, too. He took them into
the kitchen.

What? What is a sinker? You're joking, surely. Clearly,
a sinker is a lump of heavy metal,

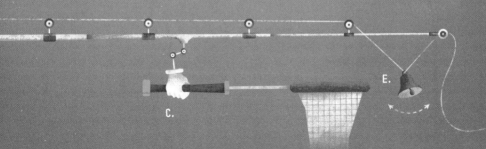

C.

E.

usually shaped like a big teardrop. Its only job, obviously enough, is to sink—to carry the hook and the bait (which are both usually very light) down into the depths of the water. Why? Because that is where the fish are.

John, you see, was quite clever when it came to mechanical things, and connecting little thingies to other thingies, and to various doodads, in order to solve certain problems. In this he was much like his father.

Abigail brought the photograph of the dog into the kitchen and joined her brother. Then the twins did a few other things, and voilà!*

The device was ready.

## QUESTIONS FOR REVIEW

1. When Cain and Abel asked Adam, their father, for a dog, and he said, "No," what was their response?

   a. "Very well, Father. You know best."
   b. "But Mom said we could!"
   c. "Please!? Please!? Please!?"

2. Which pair of words is most like the opposite of "tedious and grim"?

   a. Lively and cheerful
   b. Lettuce and tomato
   c. Lewis and Clark

3. Is this it? The twins ask for a dog and the book is over?

   a. Yes, and I am extremely upset about it, because I want to continue reading. Although of course I sympathize with the Narrator for not wanting to write any more.

   b. No, and I have no idea what will happen next, so I will happily continue reading, perhaps pausing for a moment to praise the Narrator for his superb narrating.

   c. Maybe. I shall have to see if the pages that follow are completely blank or if they have printing on them. If they do have printing on them, I shall without hesitation proceed to read it with the greatest pleasure.

*Voilà!* is French. You pronounce it "vwah-LAH." It means "Behold!" or "There you have it!" Other French words you may find yourself using in your daily life include "restaurant," "turquoise," and "France."

# CHAPTER 3

# THE TEMPLETON TWINS ASK A QUESTION

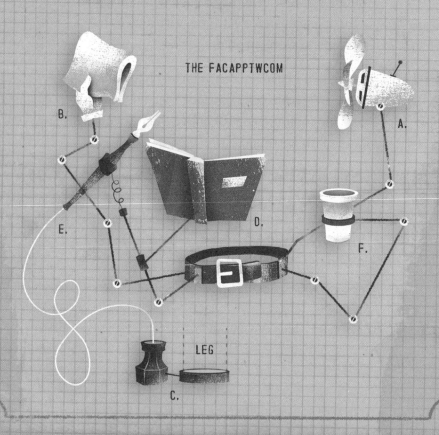

THE FACAPPTWCOM

B.

A.

E.

D.

F.

LEG

C.

**W**hen Professor Templeton emerged from his study late that afternoon, he was deep in thought, as usual. For this reason he failed to notice certain unusual things the twins had done while they were making dinner.

You heard me. They were *making* dinner. They sometimes did this, and it was no big deal to any of the Templetons. How could two twelve-year-olds do such a thing? Oh, please. They boiled water for spaghetti and heated up a jar of pasta sauce and chopped a head of lettuce into hunks and poured bottled salad dressing on it. As far as they were all concerned, this was a splendid dinner, and they had it all the time.

The Professor did not notice that the dining room table had been moved a little, and that his place had been set opposite where he usually sat. He would not have been bothered by any of these rearrangements had he been aware of them, but he wasn't. Instead, he greeted the twins in a distracted way, checked the day's mail, washed his hands, and sat down at the table.

In the kitchen, John spooned some spaghetti onto a plate, topped it with sauce, and placed some of the lettuce beside it. Then, pretending to be extremely casual and ordinary about everything, Abigail carried the plate out into the dining room and placed it before her father.

"Thank you, dear, it looks lovely," the Professor said, his mind elsewhere. By this I do not mean that the poor man's brain had been removed from his head and taken to a different location, but that he wasn't thinking about spaghetti and salad. He was thinking about other things—in fact, about an article he was reading.

You will be interested to learn that the Professor used one of his own inventions to read magazines and journals while eating. He called this invention the **Foot-Activated Compressed-Air-Powered Page-Turner with Clip-On Mount.** This, as you can see, is a perfectly dreadful name, so we'll refer to the invention as the FACAPPTWCOM.

He originally created this device for people who play the piano. It consisted of a pedal on the floor connected to a rubber hose. When you stepped on the pedal, a blast of air shot through the hose into a nozzle clipped onto the sheet music you were reading. The blast of air turned the page.

You laugh, but turning the page is an important function for piano players who read music while they're playing and who cannot lift their hands from the keys. How important is this function? It is so important that, in serious piano performances, *an entire human being* is employed to turn the pages.

I know you think I am making this up, but I assure you it is true. Ask your parent, guardian, clergyman, sports coach, or piano teacher whether or not it's true. Or don't bother with any of them, and just take my word for it.

The FACAPPTWCOM was meant to allow piano players to turn their own pages. And it worked, more or less. (Sometimes the jet of air turned more than one page, which meant the device "needed fine-tuning," but still.) Then the Professor discovered that it could also turn the pages of books and magazines, thus enabling him to eat and read at the same time *without interrupting either the eating or the reading.* He had not yet perfected the device, so it was not for sale anywhere, but he had high hopes for its success in both the piano-playing world and the reading-while-eating world.

While the Professor was reading and eating, Abigail stood there, holding her breath and sneaking glances toward the ceiling. Then she heard a sort of hissing sound and looked around.

It was John, whispering from the kitchen. "Abby! Help!"

Abigail ran into the kitchen. There was her brother holding the fishing pole. Its line ran up to and across the ceiling, crossing above the kitchen light fixture (which held it up), then ran down through the kitchen doorway, out into the dining room, and across the dining-room light fixture. It ended, finally, in the hook-and-sinker attachment, which dangled high above Professor Templeton's plate.

John pointed to the kitchen ceiling. "It's stuck."

Abigail looked: The fishing line, which John was trying to unreel, was snagged on something in the ceiling lamp. Abigail said, "Oh, for goodness' sake," and immediately placed her hands on the counter and jumped up onto it.

From her perch Abigail could see the problem. She gave the line a little jerk, and it jumped free of its snag and grew taut. John quickly reeled it in a little to keep it under control.

Abigail jumped down. "Okay," she said. "Let's go."

She dashed back out into the dining room just in time to hear her father, his eyes on his magazine, say, "Aren't you eating, children?"

And then he stopped. He realized that a photograph of a dog was descending from the ceiling directly above his plate. In fact the dog—a bright white animal with a long, pointed snout, small, flopped-over triangular ears, and lively dark eyes—was staring right at him.

"My goodness," he said.

"Papa," Abigail said. She was tense and slightly hunched over and was making the kind of ultra-careful, hold-your-breath face you make when you're walking across a frozen pond and you hope the ice won't crack beneath you.

**CAN WE GET THIS DOG?**

The Professor stared at the photograph.

"Not this very dog," Abigail said quickly. "But this type of dog. Please?"

"Please, Papa?" John called in from the kitchen.

And then, as though awakening from a dream, the Professor looked around and noticed the position of the table, which the twins had changed so that their father's place at dinner would be exactly under the light fixture. He turned and saw how the fishing line went back into the kitchen. "How very clever," he murmured.

"So, can we? Please?" Abigail said. "We'll take care of it and walk it and everything."

"Oh, I don't know, Abby," the Professor said. "A new dog . . . it's such a *change*."

"But isn't that what we need?" Abigail said.

The Professor looked at her, and at the dangling photograph of the dog, which seemed to look back at him. Then he put his fork down and thought about it.

## QUESTIONS FOR REVIEW

1. The FACAPPTWCOM works by blowing air at a book, magazine, or sheet music to turn a page. Would it work underwater? Why or why not?

2. When was the last time you played piano underwater? Write your answer here: _____

3. Why is it a good idea to call something that sinks a "sinker"? Write your answer in the form of a brief opera.

# CHAPTER 4

# INTRODUCING CASSIE, THE RIDICULOUS DOG WHO IS NOT A JACK RUSSELL

**A**s I am sure you have guessed, the Professor said something like "Oh, all right." In fact, that is exactly what he said.

"Oh, all right," he said. "Do you two know where we should get this dog?"

John and Abigail had indeed found out exactly where to get the kind of dog they wanted, and in a day or so their father drove them to a nice lady's house not far from the university, and they obtained the animal that, for reasons that are not entirely known, they named Cassie. I will refer to her by that name, too, although I will also reserve the right to refer to her as "the Ridiculous Dog."

The Ridiculous Dog was a fox terrier of the "smooth-haired" variety. (There is also a kind of fox terrier called a "wire-haired," but they look entirely different.) A smooth-haired fox terrier is a small- to medium-size dog with a long, pointy nose, two perky little triangular ears, and a tail about the length and thickness of a carrot (which fox terriers love to eat).

There is, perhaps, nothing particularly ridiculous in a dog whose appearance is as I have just described. (By the way, I suggest you try to say the words "particularly ridiculous" four times very quickly without stumbling over them. In fact I insist on it.)

It was not Cassie's appearance that made her ridiculous. It was her behavior. I don't know if you are familiar with fox terriers. You may think you are, but it is probable that the dog you think is a fox terrier is actually a Jack Russell terrier. Jack Russells (or "Jacks") are perfectly cute and so forth, but their personalities lack the essential ridiculousness of the fox terrier.

The fox terrier lives in a constant state of unbelievable and unnecessary excitement. It runs and spins and wags its little tail like a metronome that has lost its mind. When you bring out the leash to take it for a walk and you tell it to "Sit!," it proceeds to leap straight up into the air, like a dolphin in a SeaWorld show, over and over and over and over and over and over and over and over and over and over until you finally give up and say, "Oh, for goodness' sake," and you just hold it down and clip on its leash. You may do this four thousand times over the course of five years and it will never, ever sit.

The twins liked to walk Cassie, the Ridiculous Dog, around the block. One day the Professor decided to join them, and he discovered that he, too, liked to walk her around the block.

Now pay attention, please, because an important development is about to follow from this seemingly unimportant fact.

As I have mentioned, the Professor discovered that he enjoyed these walks. And why not? Each street was lined with big, old houses set back from the sidewalk, with porches that looked over gardens and hedges. Huge, ancient trees spread their heavy limbs, roofing the yards and streets in a thick canopy of leaves.

When the Professor and the twins walked the dog around the block, Cassie moved in her usual ridiculous manner, with her stiff front legs stepping briskly along and her little head alertly looking this way and that, and her little tail shaking rapidly back and forth, generally acting as though everything in the world was fascinating and electrifying and fantastic. As a result of this, people—and not only friends of the twins or of the Professor, but complete strangers—would stop to admire her.

"Is that a Jack Russell?" they would always ask.

Abigail or John would then say, "No, it's a smooth-haired fox terrier." Then the stranger or the friend and the twins and the Professor would fall into a casual, friendly conversation—about fox terriers and Jack Russells, about the specific ridiculousness of Cassie herself, or even about the weather.

Sometimes, if a stranger pointed a finger at the twins and the Professor while in friendly conversation, Cassie would think it was her job to defend the family, and she would growl. But usually she simply sat on her back legs, in that upright, I'm-being-good posture dogs sometimes adopt, until the conversation was over. After a few pleasant minutes of chat, everyone would go their separate ways.

"So what?" you might be thinking. And that's a good question. So what if people walking a dog stop and talk to other people?

But in this case, one of the people was Professor Elton Templeton, who had not yet recovered from the death of his wife, and who now, almost by accident, found himself talking to people, and getting fresh air, and enjoying the kind of pleasant, light exercise you can enjoy when walking a ridiculous dog.

This went on for about two weeks, until one morning, while the twins were bustling about getting ready to go to school, they were stunned to see their father come into the kitchen dressed in a sparkling new billowy white shirt and crisp, if baggy, white pants. "I'll be in my office until four, children," he said. "Don't worry about dinner. I'll bring something back."

Abigail asked, "You'll be in the office?"

"The office at the university?" John added.

The Professor replied quite casually, as though it were the most natural thing in the world, "Why, yes. I'm going back to work."

The twins were delighted to hear this. They would have leapt up and cried, "Yay!" and "All ri-i-i-ght!" and given each other high-fives and then grinningly descended on their father for a triumphant three-way hug, except for the fact that such things only happen on television and in the movies. Instead, Abigail said, "That's superb, Papa!" and John said, "Wow. Okay!" and the Professor smiled a shy little smile, picked up his briefcase, and left.

Isn't that wonderful? (Hint: Yes, it is.) Thanks to the ordinary, everyday act of walking a dog, the Professor found a way to get out of his workshop, out of his study, out of the house, really, out of *himself*, and back into the world. This did not mean that he no longer missed his wife. It meant that he could miss his wife but still get on with the rest of his life.

Or so he thought.

That very afternoon, the twins returned home from school and puttered around in the kitchen, making some silly after-school snack, such as cream cheese on apples, or celery stuffed with graham crackers, or whatever it is that children seem to like.

Suddenly, and to their surprise, a figure appeared in the kitchen doorway. Cassie barked at the intruder until John told her to be quiet. Because it was no intruder. It was their father. He was holding a large pizza box, and he looked tired and unhappy.

"You're home early, Papa," Abigail said. "Is something wrong?"

"Children," he said. "We . . . ah, that is to say, I think . . .

## WE . . . WE ARE GOING TO HAVE TO MOVE.

The twins were shocked.

"You mean, to a new house?" John asked.

"Yes, I mean, I, ah . . . Yes, dear, to a new house," the Professor said. "But not just that. To a new university and a new town. A new . . . everything. I have accepted a post at the Tickeridge-Baltock Institute of Technology."

"Tick-Tock Tech?" Abigail asked. "Why?" It was typical of Abigail to have heard and remembered the nickname of the Tickeridge-Baltock Institute of Technology, wasn't it? Just say, "Yes, it was." Because it was.

"They are providing me with resources for completing my work on my Personal

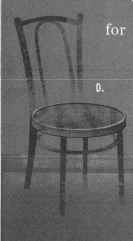

D.

One-Man Helicopter," the Professor said. "Tickeridge-Baltock will provide me with a laboratory and money and so forth."

"But doesn't the university give you those things, too?" Abigail asked. "Why do we have to move?"

At this the Professor looked uncomfortable and unhappy. He said, "Because we do. And that is that." He handed the pizza box to John and went into his study.

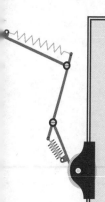

## QUESTIONS FOR REVIEW

1. Mary has five oranges. She gives two to Tom. Tom then buys twice as many as Mary has left and gives half of them to her. Who cares?

2. Why are some dogs ridiculous, whereas other dogs are utterly ridiculous?

3. Have you ever walked around the block? Would you like to do so now? The rest of us will wait here until you return. *Or will we?*

# CHAPTER 5

# THE TEMPLETONS (AND THEIR RIDICULOUS DOG) TAKE A TERRIFIC AND TIMELY TOUR OF TICK-TOCK TECH

It took about a month for the Templetons to pack up their belongings and get ready to move. During this time there were little articles in newspapers and magazines announcing Professor Templeton's transfer to the Tickeridge-Baltock Institute of Technology. When the faculty and administration and students at Elysian University learned that the Professor would be leaving, they held a big farewell party for him.

All of this affection and respect made the Templeton twins wonder more than ever why their father felt it necessary to move. But whenever they asked him, he gave some vague answer, and finally they just stopped asking.

Finally moving day arrived. A huge truck pulled up in front of the Templetons' front door, and three men lugged the family's furniture and boxes out of the house and into the truck. Cassie naturally felt it was a good idea to bark constantly—and ridiculously—at these men until John put her in a room and shut the door. (The Ridiculous Dog barked in there, too, but it wasn't as annoying.)

When the moving van was loaded up, the Templetons drove behind it to the little town where the Tickeridge-Baltock Institute of Technology (which we *may* sometimes refer to, not only as "Tick-Tock Tech," but "TBIT") was located. The van went on to the Templetons' new house. The family drove to the institute.

"Isn't it marvelous!" their father said as they pulled into the main driveway. They came to a stop in front of a grand brick building with tall white columns on either side of its entrance. Nearby hung a sign that read

## COLONEL HALL (ADMINISTRATION)

"Where is everybody?" Abigail said.

The twins had lived all their lives on college campuses, and Abigail knew how busy and bustling such places always were, as students and teachers and visitors and staff walked and jogged and lounged around in the yards and on the benches. Now she spun around and looked in every direction. She gestured toward the grassy quad that stretched out before them—and, since a quad is a four-sided space surrounded by buildings, it was quite convenient for her to point to the other buildings nearby, as well. Not one single person was walking or lounging or jogging or lounging. The place was deserted.

The Professor looked up at the giant clock atop the roof of Colonel Hall. (By the way, if you are reading this aloud to yourself or to others, and if you have pronounced the name of this building as "ko-LOW-nel Hall" or "KAHL-un-ull Hall," you are in error. "Colonel" is pronounced "KER-null." A colonel is an officer in the Army. I know—exactly where is the "r" in "colonel"? Why should we say "KER-null" when there's no "r"? Believe me, I deplore it as much as you do—and I'm an adult, and I'm used to it. It's outrageous. **LET'S MOVE ON.**)

"It's quarter to the hour," the Professor said after looking at the clock atop KER-null Hall. "The students must all be in class. As they should be!" Then he said, "Let's take a look around."

Colleges, as you may know, usually have a number of buildings, each dedicated to a particular department or other specific use, and most of them are named this-or-that "hall." TBIT was no different. As the Templeton twins and their father drove slowly around the campus, they saw a sign at the entrance of each building that announced its name and its department. The twins and their father drove past Fawn Hall (headquarters of the communications department), Annie Hall (performing arts), Donald Hall (English), and Monty Hall (business administration studies).*

It was as they drove past Jim and Daryl Hall (music department) that the twins noticed an odd thing. At other universities, perhaps one building in each cluster has a clock as part of its architecture. But at Tick-Tock Tech, *every* building had a massive, grand tower on its roof and every tower had a huge clock. Some of the clock faces had regular numerals, while others had Roman numerals. Some had sweeping second hands, while others did not. But all showed exactly the same time.

In addition, big pieces of sculpture stood here and there on the grassy areas in front of various buildings, and each of them depicted something having to do with the measurement of time: a slowly moving pendulum, a stainless-steel set of interlocking gears, a giant wristwatch, an interesting construction of large brass springs.

---

*It is true that there are famous people, whom your parents or guardians may have heard of, named Fawn Hall, Annie Hall, Donald Hall, and Monty Hall. But these buildings *obviously* were not named after them. If they had been, they would have been named Fawn Hall Hall, Annie Hall Hall, and so forth.

The hedges had all been trimmed into those toothlike patterns (called crenellations) you see in clock gears (and on castles—in fact, they are the castle-y looking things that tell you, "this is a castle"). Even the leaves of the trees seemed to move in a crisp back-and-forth, tick-tock motion. It all felt very orderly and calm, as though the world were moving at a steady, even, unchanging rhythm.

Then the twins heard a sharp, loud noise—a combined clack and slam and bang—coming from many different directions all around them. Each clock, at the same moment, was making its own special two o'clock noise. Some chimed the familiar ding-dong/ding-dong tune. Others just chimed twice, deeply and loudly. On one building, a pair of doors under the clock swung open and, to the sound of gnashing gears and stuttering machinery and creaking wood, out came an enormous mechanical cuckoo, who cuckooed enormously, twice. From the music building came a rippling pattern of bells that ended in two triumphant bongs.

Abigail and John traded a look that said, "Wow." One of them may have been about to say something out loud, but suddenly all the doors of all the buildings flew open, and, before they knew it, the quad was boiling with commotion and noise.

Hundreds of students swarmed around them, talking and laughing and yelling and teasing and punching and slapping and crying and singing and giggling and arguing as they moved to their next classes in tick-tock marching steps toward every building in sight.

One by one, like seconds ticking off, the students marched into the front doors of the various buildings until they were all inside. All the doors of all the buildings banged shut at once with a giant, resounding SLAM! that echoed into silence around the quad. Once again, the entire college seemed deserted.

Abigail began to say something—but her brother suddenly tapped her hard on the shoulder. She spun and saw him holding up a finger, meaning, "Shh." Then he pointed off to the side.

At the intersection of several concrete walking paths stood a little sheltered bulletin board of the kind many colleges have all over campus for the posting of public announcements and advertisements. It was covered with notices about lost cats and offers of guitar lessons and ads for dramatic productions and information about clubs to join and movies to see and concerts to attend and all the other events and services that might interest students at a big college.

Most conspicuous among them, pinned front and center, was a poster featuring a photograph of their father.

John gave his sister a look that said, wordlessly, "Good grief, that's the most shockingly awful thing I've ever seen, and I can't possibly imagine who put it there or why!"

Abigail gave him a return look that replied, silently, "It's completely horrible and outrageous, and we should make it our business to find out who did this and set him or her straight!"

The poster welcomed "famed inventor Prof. Elton Templeton" as a visiting fellow at TBIT and invited the public to a lecture the Professor would give a few nights later on the subject of "Personal Transport Modalities and the Problem of Linkage."

That, in and of itself, was not terrible. It was actually kind of nice. No, what was terrible was that someone had scrawled, in thick, ferocious black letters across their father's picture, the word **"THIEF"**!!!!!!

TBIT *invites the public to the lecture of*

# TEMPLETON

*discussing*

PTWST

AND THE

PROBLEM OF LINKAGE

TWIST

FAMED
*inventor*

NIGHT
only

### SELF
EDITING
PENCIL

2

### BATTERY
POWERED
### TOOTH
PICK

4

### POOCH
POWERED
### POOPY
PINCHER

3

1

BEGINS AT 8PM

The twins both looked at their father. He was gazing across the lovely landscape and seemed not to have noticed the poster. "Let's go to the house!" Abigail said with what I must tell you was a bit of fake excitement.

"Yeah!" John said, also with phony enthusiasm. "So we can unpack!"

Professor Templeton was somewhat surprised at the twins' sudden desire to go to the house, but he said, "Yes, all right," and the family drove off before he could see the poster and its nasty addition.

## QUESTIONS FOR REVIEW

1. Why do you think someone would scrawl the word "THIEF" on a picture of nice Professor Templeton?

2. Isn't it silly to try to answer Question 1? Shouldn't you just keep your "theories" to yourself and continue reading?

3. True or false (circle one): The Narrator is a wonderful person.        T        T

## CHAPTER 6

# THE
# HANDSOME
# MAN

The Templeton twins' new home was a worn but comfortable old-fashioned house of dark gray wood. Cracked, weathered shutters framed the windows and made them look like intelligent, squinting eyes. There was a nice porch in the front and a small, fenced-in backyard in which Cassie could bark at squirrels in a ridiculous fashion.

Two nights after they had moved in, following an early dinner, Professor Templeton said, "Well, I'm off to give my lecture. Would you two like to come along?"

Now, neither John nor Abigail was particularly interested in "personal transport modalities" or "the problem of linkage." In fact, they didn't know what any of that meant. Neither do you, of course, and—although this will surprise you—neither do I. But the twins were excited at the idea that their father would be in front of an audience, so they happily said yes, they'd love to join him.

They accompanied the Professor to the biggest auditorium at the institute, in Jim and Daryl Hall. When they got there, they were happy to see that a good crowd of students, teachers, and local people from the town had assembled to hear the Professor speak. The twins sat in the front row and felt very proud of their father.

It is possible you have heard of some of Professor Elton Templeton's inventions. He invented the **Battery-Operated Toothpick** (also known as the **BOT**), the **Self-Adjusting Chromatic Shoehorn** (the so-called **SACS**), the **Husk-Removing Garlic Press** (which cooks refer to as the **HRGP**), the **Adjust-O-Matic Diving Board** (known informally as the **AOMDB**), and the **Self-Tensioning Book Ends** (the **STB**, beloved of librarians throughout the universe). To the students and teachers at TBIT (most of whom were, or wanted to be, engineers and inventors, too), Professor Templeton was a star, and the audience for his lecture that evening was big, happy, and excited.

On the stage was a stand with a little light and a microphone. Behind it was a huge white screen. A young man introduced the Professor and everyone applauded. The twins were thrilled. *Thrilled.* The Professor thanked everyone, and then the lights went down. As he stood at the stand and spoke into the microphone, a series of pictures of his inventions, his sketches, and his calculations appeared on the screen.

Finally, to conclude the lecture, the Professor spoke about his current invention, the **Personal One-Man Helicopter** (the **POMH**).

This was a device you strapped onto your back, like a knapsack, and it held a motor, controls, and those fanlike turning things that are called rotors. The Personal One-Man Helicopter allowed the person using it to fly both up and down and over distances. Such a device, the Professor hoped, would eliminate the need for many cars, and would help people get to where they were going faster and more cheaply.

John and Abigail knew all about this invention, of course, because their father had discussed it with them over the years, and asked their opinions about it, and shown them his drawings. So the things he told the audience were not new to them. But they enjoyed hearing the audience laugh and applaud for their father when he said a funny or clever thing. When the lecture was over, Professor Templeton asked the audience if they had any questions.

Four or five people asked about the different problems the Professor was trying to solve so that the **POMH** would work safely and not be too expensive to produce. The Professor answered the questions and people applauded again.

Then a man raised his hand and stood up. He was six feet tall, beautifully dressed in an elegantly tailored black suit, a bright white shirt, and a pale blue tie, and very handsome. In fact, wherever he went, people could be heard whispering to each other, "My, what a handsome man!"

"Yes?" Professor Templeton said. "Do you have a question?"

"I have several questions, Professor Elton Templeton," the man said. "My first question is, don't you recognize me?"

The Professor frowned, squinted at the man, and shielded his eyes from the stage lights, but finally shook his head. "I'm afraid I don't recognize you," he said. "Is there any reason I should?"

"Oh, yes, there is every reason you should," the man said. "But let me ask my next question. My next question is:

**HOW DARE YOU?!**

The people in the audience gasped. Abigail and John gave each other a look that said wordlessly, "Yikes!"

Professor Templeton looked puzzled. "How dare I what?" he said.

"How dare you pretend that the Personal One-Man Helicopter is *your* invention?" the man said angrily. "When you know full well it is really *my* idea!"

The Professor became even more confused. "Well, I, I mean to say," he stammered. "I don't think the idea for a one-person aerial transportation device is *any* one person's idea. Many different people have had similar ideas over the years."

"This one is mine!"

"But, I mean to say, people have been talking about one-person jetpacks for fifty years," the Professor went on. "I mean, my goodness, Leonardo da Vinci himself drew sketches of a one-man helicopter over five hundred years ago."

"Not like mine!" the handsome man yelled. "My idea was, put it in a knapsack. That's what I told you. Put it in a knapsack!"

"Oh, but that is quite impossible. We have never even met."

THE TEMPLETON TWINS HAVE AN IDEA

"We have indeed met, sir." The handsome man extended one beautifully jacketed arm and pointed a sharp, stabbing finger at Professor Templeton. "When you were my professor at Elysian University thirteen years ago!"

At this everyone in the room fell completely silent. If there had been a band in the auditorium, it would have played something stern and dramatic, such as **"DUM-DUM-DUMMMMMM!"** All eyes were on Professor Templeton as he stared hard at the handsome man. The Professor thought and thought and thought until finally he said, "Are you Mr. Dean?"

"I am!" the handsome man said with an attitude of triumph. **"I AM DEAN D. DEAN!"**

The Professor nodded. Then he said, "Mr. Dean, you may or you may not have told me to put it in a knapsack thirteen years ago. I don't remember."

"Well, I do!"

"But what you must remember is that it is very common for different people to have the same idea. It happens all the time."

"I said, 'Put it in a knapsack!'"

"What matters," the Professor said, now speaking to the crowd and looking directly at the twins in the front row, "is not what ideas you have, but what you do with your ideas."

The audience clapped at this very wise observation. The twins applauded as hard as they could. But the handsome man waved his arms wildly around until everyone fell silent again.

"Oh, really?" he said. "Oh, is that so? Oh, is that the case?"

"Well, yes," the Professor said. "It is."

"Look, Professor," said Dean D. Dean. "Just because your wife died and everyone feels sorry for you doesn't mean I didn't say 'Put it in a knapsack' thirteen years ago!"

The audience was astounded. Everyone felt that it was extremely rude and even nasty for Dean D. Dean to mention the Professor's wife in that way. Finally the Professor said, "I will tell you what I do remember about you, Mr. Dean. You are the only student to whom I have ever given a failing grade."

"You stole my ideas!"

"I did no such thing. I don't steal ideas. First, because it is unethical. Second, because I have plenty of ideas of my own."

The audience burst into applause and cheers, and the young man who had introduced the Professor came out onto the stage, stood beside the Professor, and, looking at Dean D. Dean, said into the microphone, "Sir? We're going to have to ask you to leave the auditorium."

The audience applauded even more. Dean D. Dean became extremely angry. He again pointed a finger at the Professor and yelled,

**THIS ISN'T OVER, PROFESSOR ELTON TEMPLETON!**

With a snort, he forced his way past all the people sitting in his row without even saying, "Excuse me" or "Sorry." ("My, what a handsome man," someone whispered. "But so rude!") Then he marched furiously up the aisle and out of the auditorium.

For a moment everyone was silent. Then Professor Templeton said, quietly, "Well, I imagine that concludes tonight's presentation." At this the entire audience leapt to its feet and applauded and whistled and cheered. The Professor thanked them with a little nod and a wave. He caught the eyes of Abigail and John and nodded to them, too.

Naturally, with all this drama and excitement (and rudeness), people couldn't wait to swarm toward the stage to meet the Professor, to ask about his inventions, and to tell him how terrible Dean D. Dean had been.

While waiting for their father, Abigail said to John, "That Dean D. Dean must be the one who wrote 'thief' on Papa's picture."

John nodded. "I wonder what he meant when he said that this wasn't over."

What he meant, as we shall see, was that this wasn't over.

## QUESTIONS FOR REVIEW

1. Do you think it is really possible for different people to have the same idea at the same time?

2. You do? But I was about to say that I do, too. Is this a coincidence, or have you stolen my idea?

   a. It is a coincidence.
   b. I have stolen the Narrator's idea.
   c. The Narrator has stolen *my* idea.
   d. All of the above.

3. This isn't over. (That isn't actually a question. I'll rephrase.) You do know that this isn't over, don't you?

CHAPTER 7

D.

CRUM
CAST
SPIN
DRY.

CRAZY!

(8, 3, 5)

A | t nine o'clock the next morning, just as the chimes and bongs and cuckoos of the university clocks were fading into silence, the doorbell rang. When Abigail, John, the Professor, and Cassie (barking ridiculously as usual) answered the door, they beheld a tall, thin woman in gray pants and a gray shirt and a black baseball cap.

"Ah!" the Professor said. He consulted a sheet of paper he had brought with him. "Are you . . . Nancy Noonan?"

"Who else would I be?" the woman said, and marched straight into the house. It was hard to tell how old she was. She wore no makeup, and when she stuck out her hand for a good, honest shake, you could see that she cut her nails short and wore no polish. "Call me Nan."

The Professor shook her hand and then introduced Abigail and John. "This is your new nanny," he said.

**CALL ME NANNY NAN.**

The new nanny shook hands with each twin. "I'll tell you right now that I don't like twins. They think they can *get away* with things. But! Don't you worry. That's my problem."

THE TEMPLETON TWINS HAVE AN IDEA

John looked a bit confused as he said, "Um . . . nice to meet you. . . ."

Abigail frowned. "Your name is Nanny Nan Noonan?"

"Ding! You got it!" The tall, brisk woman clapped her hands together. "Okay! Let's unpack!" She turned and started to march up the stairs, then suddenly stopped, looked down at the twins, and held out a long, skinny finger. "Just don't try to *get away* with anything."

Immediately Cassie started to snarl at Nanny Nan. As John told the dog, "No!" and dragged her away from the stairs, Abigail explained, "We're sorry. She gets angry if someone points a finger at us. She thinks they're going to attack us."

"Well, she's got me all wrong! I'm not attacking anybody," the nanny said. "At least not today."

And, while the twins tried to decide whether or not Nanny Nan was joking, she went upstairs.

Nanny Nan was strong and tireless. She opened cartons. She moved dressers and desks and chests of drawers into just the right position. She told John and Abigail exactly where to store their clothes—what drawers to put their socks or shirts in, where and exactly how to position their shoes, and so on.

Of course, the twins did tell her that, while the house might have been new to them, the dressers and chests of drawers were the same ones they had lived with all their lives, and that they already knew where to put their own clothes and shoes. But she insisted they do it her way. "No one keeps their shirts in the bottom drawer," Nanny Nan said firmly.

"I do," John said.

"Oh, nonsense," said Nanny Nan, and that was that.

Finally, when all the clothes had been put away and everyone was exhausted, Nanny Nan made a somewhat frightening chicken dish for dinner. Then the Professor went down into the basement to arrange his workshop, and John and Abigail went to their rooms to lovingly unpack the things they used for their hobbies.

You no doubt wish me to tell you what those hobbies were. And I shall. But first let us be clear about what a "hobby" is and what it is not.

A hobby, which is an old-fashioned word people don't use much anymore, refers to something you do

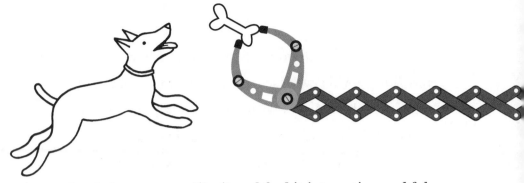

*simply because you like it and find it interesting and ful-filling.* You don't get paid to do it. You don't get extra credit in school for doing it. You don't do it because it might impress your friends or look good when you apply for university or a job. You don't do it because it might be good for your health. You don't do it to save money or time. You don't do it to save the Earth. You don't do it to save the whales.

And you certainly don't do it because other people force you to—as, for example, they might force you to write a book about the Templeton twins.

No, you pursue your hobby (or hobbies) because you like it (or them). This is no small thing. Ask any grown-up you know about his or her hobby and—assuming they have one—they will talk enthusiastically to you about it for the next twelve hours. Then the next day they'll call you up and start talking about it again.

You will be delighted to know that I have a hobby, too. But we will save discussion of what my hobby is for later on in this story, or perhaps for a different story altogether, or perhaps for never. I may decide I don't want to discuss my hobby with you. Because why should I? What have you ever done for me?

## LET'S MOVE ON.

Abigail's hobby was crossword puzzles—but of a rather special kind.

I assume you know what a regular crossword puzzle is, so I'm not going to describe it to you. Let's just say that you have a big box filled with little empty boxes, and you're given a series of clues about which words will correctly fill in the empty boxes. The words intersect with one another. So, for example, filling in one word across gives you a letter in a different word—or many letters in many words—going down.

All right, I see I have done what I said I wasn't going to do. I have described regular crossword puzzles. Well, you can thank me later.

The problem with regular crossword puzzles is not that some are too hard. Working on hard puzzles can be fun, in a satisfying kind of way. Or it can be annoying, in which case you just stop and do something else.

No, the real problem comes when puzzles are too easy.

If the clues are too straightforward and the answers are too obvious, then doing the crossword puzzle becomes a tedious kind of work. You don't stop (because it's easy to fill in), but it's not satisfying. It's like filling in a form to apply for membership in an extremely boring club that you don't really want to join in the first place.

The trick, then, is to find puzzles that are neither too easy nor too hard.

(Yes, yes, I know: The same is true about books. We want to read books that are neither too easy nor too hard. Kindly do not bother me with your request that this book be one of those. It should be enough that I'm writing it at all. Now, where were we? No, don't tell me. Let me guess. Ah, yes: crossword puzzles.)

Abigail Templeton was one of those clever people who found regular crossword puzzles too easy and rather tedious. So instead her hobby was doing *cryptic* crossword puzzles.

"Cryptics," as people refer to them, are different from ordinary crossword puzzles. They have squares to fill in with words, and the words intersect across and down, as in a normal crossword. But the clues are . . .

Well, let us just say that the clues can seem absurd. But once you learn how to read them, and what the basic rules of cryptic crosswords are, you will see that the clues are actually little puzzles in themselves. You have to figure out what the clue means before you can even guess at the word.

That's the bad news. The good news is, much of the time *the answer to everything is right in front of your nose.*

For example, one of the clues in the first cryptic that Abigail tried to solve was this:

# CRAZY HEN TICK MEANS A HOT ROOM (7).

I know: It looks like it makes no sense. What is a "hen tick"? What does it mean for a hen tick to be crazy? How can it mean a hot room? This clue seemed a deliberate attempt to make the person doing the puzzle throw it out the window.

But here is how Abigail figured out this clue.

First, the number at the end told her that the answer was one word with seven letters. (Sometimes the answers are two or three words. Then there are two or three numbers, indicating the number of letters in each word.)

Second, she knew that a clue like "crazy" (or "mixedup," "changed," "weird," "insane," "odd," "loopy," "nuts," "broken," "smashed," "exploded," and so on) meant that she should rearrange the letters in the nearby word or words in the clue into the correct answer.

Therefore it was possible, she decided, that if she rearranged "hen tick" (which, she realized in a burst of happiness, has seven letters), the answer would have something to do with "means a hot room."

So she looked at "hen tick," jumbled those letters up in her head, and rearranged them into

| K | I | T | C | H | E | N |
|---|---|---|---|---|---|---|

Did that "mean a hot room"? Yes, because a kitchen can indeed be a hot room. So KITCHEN was the right answer.

Now that you know how this works, go back and look at the title of this chapter again. See if you can figure out what it really means by getting "crazy" with those letters. The answer—which I urge you not to look at until you at least try to figure it out—is down below.*

Abigail unpacked her hobby equipment, which included several books of puzzles, a dictionary, and a pad of blank paper for trying out combinations of letters. And, as long as she had all this stuff in front of her, she decided to do a puzzle.

She sat at her desk and turned on the desk lamp. In working on her puzzles, by the way, she had the benefit of one of her father's many inventions: the Self-Generating Variable Luminosity Light Pen, or SGVLLP.

---

*The answer, as the numbers plainly inform you, is three words, of eight, three, and five letters. Try asking yourself, "What is a very common three-letter word that might appear in a chapter title?" The obvious two answers to that are "and" and "the." Since there is no "h" or "e" in the title, it can't be "the." So try eliminating "AND" from the cryptic title, and rearrange what is left. You will end up with the word CRYPTICS and the word DRUMS. Now put the "and" back and there you have it: CRYPTICS AND DRUMS.

THE TEMPLETON TWINS HAVE AN IDEA

Okay, we can all agree that Professor Templeton was not skilled at naming his inventions. But he was skilled at inventing his inventions, and this was one of them. It was a pen attached by a thin black cord to a band you wore around your head. On the band was a light that shined down on whatever you were writing. The clever part of this invention was that the brightness of the light increased with the motion of the pen. So when you were writing, the light was bright. When you stopped writing and were thinking, the light was dim.

Abigail had been working away at the puzzle for about fifteen minutes when she heard a sharp knock on her bedroom door. Before she could say, "Who is it?" or "Come in," the door creaked open and Nanny Nan appeared. She was still wearing her black baseball cap. She had worn it during dinner, too.

"Too quiet in here," Nanny Nan said. "I don't like it when a kid's room is quiet. It means they're probably trying to *get away* with something."

"I'm doing a cryptic crossword," Abigail said. "It's my hobby."

"Oh, baloney," the nanny sniffed. "That's not a hobby. Crossword puzzles are for grown-ups to do on a train. A hobby for a kid is collecting stamps or building plastic models of ships and airplanes."

Nanny Nan marched over to Abigail and picked up the cryptic crossword book. "Hmm," she said, skimming it quickly. "No, I don't like the look of this. 'Sneak nuts into cobra, five.' It makes me nervous. No one would try to sneak nuts into a cobra unless she was trying to *get away* with something."

Abigail brightened. "SNAKE!"

Nanny Nan's eyes widened. "Where?!" She grabbed Abigail's pen and peered wildly around the room. "Stand back!"

"No," Abigail said. She gently took the puzzle book from Nanny Nan and pointed at the open page. "'Sneak nuts into cobra' is a clue. And the answer has five letters. The word 'sneak' is *nuts*. That means you rearrange the letters of 'sneak.' You can move them around and get 'snake.' A cobra *is* a snake—and it has five letters. So the answer is SNAKE!"

"I don't like snakes. And I don't like the idea of sneaking nuts anywhere. If you have nuts, eat them. Period. Now read a book."

"But if I read, the room will be quiet and you'll come in and think I am trying to *get away* with something," Abigail said.

"That's right," replied Nanny Nan. "And that's why I want you to read out loud." Nanny Nan shook her head, tucked the crossword puzzle book under her arm, and headed for the door. **"OUT LOUD!"** she called over her shoulder as she left.

Meanwhile, in his room, John had lovingly taken the equipment for his hobby out of its cases.

Yes, "cases." John, you see, played the drums.

His set of drums, as drum sets go, was basic but complete. He had a bass drum that sat on the floor and, with the use of a foot pedal, made a deep, booming sound. He had a high-hat stand, which also worked by a pedal

and which brought two small cymbals together with a nice CHIKK sound. He also had a snare drum, which was a thin drum with a lot of tightly coiled wires running across its bottom head that made a crisp marching sound. He had two tom-toms, which had no wires running across their bottom heads and made a deeper, familiar drum sound.

John also had two larger cymbals, each mounted on its own stand, that made different kinds of shimmering and crashy sounds, and a stool to sit on while playing—which is exactly what he was doing, quite happily, when the door to his room flew open and a very exasperated Nanny Nan strode in and waved her arms for quiet. He stopped playing.

**"TOO NOISY!"** she shouted. "I don't like it when a kid's room is too noisy. It means they're probably trying to *get away* with something!"

"I'm practicing the drums," John explained. "It's my hobby."

"AGAIN with the hobby," the nanny said. "No. Out of the question. Go build an airplane or a ship. Out loud!" And with that she strode from the room.

I am drawing your attention to the twins' hobbies because they will prove to be *extremely important* to this story (and, for all I know, other stories), so file them in the back of your mind for future reference.

I say this although I have no idea what it actually means. How do you file something in the back of your, or anyone's, mind? So pretend I didn't say this. I will remind you of these hobbies, and their importance, over and over again anyway. So don't bother filing anything, and just leave the back of your mind alone.

A moment later, as John was sitting on the drum stool wondering what to do next, the door opened and his sister walked in.

**THIS IS TERRIBLE,** she said.

## QUESTIONS FOR REVIEW

1. See if you can solve this cryptic clue. (Hint: The answer is the name of a wonderful person.) *Insane rant roar! (8)*

2. Since playing the drums requires using both your hands and both your feet at the same time, it is physically impossible. Therefore, no one can play the drums. The same is true of driving a car, swimming, and dancing. None of these activities can be performed by human beings. Discuss.

3. Would you like Nanny Nan Noonan to be *your* nanny? Well, maybe it isn't up to you.

CHAPTER 8

# A VISIT FROM
# A MYSTERIOUS
# VISITOR!

T he next day the Professor wanted to show the twins his new laboratory, so late in the afternoon he drove them to the campus of Tick-Tock Tech. Nothing more had been said about Dean D. Dean and his very rude behavior at the lecture, and everyone was in a fine mood.

The Professor and the Templeton twins walked past the various buildings and the hedges trimmed into their squared-off, gear-tooth patterns and the sculptures of watches and pendulums and springs. They paused before a broad, grassy quad that was completely deserted and silent.

Suddenly they heard, from every direction, all the hour hands on all the tower clocks reaching the number four. Chimes, bells, and cuckoos all chimed, rang, and cuckooed four times—at which point the doors of the different buildings banged open and hundreds of students swarmed outside.

Then the twins and their father saw something they had never seen before.

While some students marched across the quad and into other buildings for their next class, many others were finished with their classes for the day and remained outside for recreation or simply to loaf around.

What do college students do when they remain outside for recreation or simply to loaf around? They throw Frisbees (those colorful plastic disks) back and forth. And that's what these students did. But they did it in a way that can be seen only at the Tickeridge-Baltock Institute of Technology.

The students throwing Frisbees stood around the outer edges of the big, open quad, and they all threw their Frisbees at exactly the same time and at the same speed. From every direction, at the same moment, the Frisbees all criss-crossed in mid-air, just barely missing one another. Then they continued down toward the people they had been thrown to. Those people caught them, aimed, and threw them—all at the same time, from every direction—up toward the same spot in the air.

"Remarkable," Professor Templeton said.

The Templetons continued on their way. They were just about to enter Jerry Hall (headquarters of the physics and physical systems department) when their progress was blocked by a man in a smooth, perfectly cut, dark blue suit and deep red tie.

It was Dean D. Dean. He not only looked handsome, he was smiling.

"Good afternoon!" he said. "Isn't it a nice day?"

"It is, yes," the Professor said carefully. "Mr. Dean, I don't think it's appropriate for you to speak with me."

"Please," Dean D. Dean said. "Call me Dean."

"What do you want?" John asked.

"Now, John," the Professor said. "That isn't polite."

"After the bad things he said about you the other night," Abigail said, "why should we be polite to him?"

"And these must be the twins!" Dean D. Dean said with a big, big smile. "The ones who were born the very day we were discussing my grade, Professor!" Dean D. Dean bent down toward the twins, who looked at him with squinty eyes of mistrust and frowning, suspicious mouths. "Isn't this nice?" he said in the tone of someone who did not really think it was nice.

"Mr. Dean," the Professor said. "How is it that you are here? Are you a student at the institute?"

Dean D. Dean looked into the eyes of John and Abigail with an expression that, for one second, was without any smile whatsoever. It looked like a warning. Then he stood up and resumed smiling.

"How is it that I am here? Am I a student at the institute?" Dean D. Dean gave out a big laugh that, to the twins at least, sounded fake. "Wuh-HA-ha-ha! My word, no! No, I could never be a student at any decent university again! Not after receiving that F you gave me!"

"As I said at the time, you have only yourself to blame," the Professor said. "Now excuse us." Professor Templeton took John and Abigail's hands and attempted to escort them into the lab building.

But Dean D. Dean blocked their way. "Oh, but don't go yet!" he said. "Surely you want to know why I'm here, Professor. You see, I read in a magazine that you were moving here to Clip-Clop Tech—"

"It's Tick-Tock," Abigail said.

"Oh, please, fine, yes, you moved here to Tick-Tock Town to resume work on our helicopter—"

"Tick-Tock TECH!"

The Professor frowned. "Our helicopter . . .?"

"—so I packed my things and I moved here, too! So we could work together!"

Dean D. Dean sidled over and leaned his head close to the Professor's and said softly, "So come on, Elton. What do you say? Let's let bygones be bygones. You just admit that I was the one who told you to put the helicopter in a knapsack, you share the credit and the money with me, and we'll be friends again!"

"Out of the question," the Professor said. He moved past Dean D. Dean and steered the twins through the front door. "We were never friends and never shall be. Now stand back, sir."

IT'S NOT FAIR! Dean D. Dean shouted. "Those twins are the reason I flunked out of college! If they hadn't been born, I would have gotten you to give me a C! I should hate them! In fact I DO hate them!" Then he stopped shouting, calmed down, and smiled. "But if you simply share the invention with me, I won't hate them anymore, and everyone will be happy!"

The Professor followed the twins through the front door and shut it. When they came out, about an hour later, Dean D. Dean was gone.

The twins had chattered excitedly while the Professor showed them around his office and his laboratory, but once everyone was in the car and on the way to the house, they quieted down. The Professor didn't notice.

But we have noticed, haven't we? And we know why the twins fell silent and got moody. They were worried about Dean D. Dean and wondered what he would do next. And, frankly, they weren't crazy about the idea of going home to Nanny Nan Noonan and her gray clothes and black baseball cap and all her bossy rules. Well, tough. Sometimes life isn't fair, as I know all too well.

Dinner that evening was meatloaf, and while it wasn't the greatest meatloaf in the history of the world, it wasn't bad. Abigail and John asked if they could have ketchup on theirs. Nanny Nan forced a tight smile and said, "But it doesn't need ketchup." Then she suggested that eating meatloaf with ketchup was "childish."

"It *is* childish," John said.

"We're children," Abigail said. "Children like ketchup with meatloaf."

It goes without saying that, during this meal, Cassie the Ridiculous Dog sat beside John's chair, her pointy nose directed at his plate, her bright, insane eyes staring at his food. Every so often she shifted a little, as though expecting that, at any moment now, something important would happen.

And then something important did happen.

The doorbell rang. Professor Templeton got up and went to answer it. He opened the front door, and the twins heard a now-familiar voice say, "Hello, Professor. I hope I'm not disturbing you."

"As a matter of fact, you are, Mr. Dean," the Professor said.

The twins traded a look that said, wordlessly, "Uh-oh, that creepy Dean D. Dean is here, with his horrible laugh and his phony smile, and there's no telling what he'll do, so let's see if we can help Papa get rid of him."

They both jumped up and ran to the door, and Nanny Nan followed. They arrived just as Dean D. Dean said, "Then I'll be brief," and walked into the hallway. He was wearing the beautiful dark blue suit and red tie he had worn earlier that day, and he was holding an old wire-bound notebook. "I have proof, you see," he said.

"Proof of what?" the Professor asked.

"Why, proof about the Personal One-Man Helicopter, of course," Dean D. Dean said. "I have proof that I was the one who said, 'Put it in a knapsack.'"

"Oh, what nonsense," the Professor said.

**"WUH-HA-HA-HA,"** Dean D. Dean fake-laughed. "We'll see what nonsense is!"

And with that he opened the notebook and shoved it into the face of Professor Templeton. "I believe this will serve as all the proof any reasonable person needs," he said.

The Professor put on his glasses, which hung from a chain around his neck, and examined the notebook.

Suddenly everyone heard a noise from the dining room. Now, when there is food on a dinner table and a dog in the dining room and no people to monitor the dog, almost any noise is a bad sign. (Interestingly, sometimes *no noise whatsoever* can also be a bad sign.)

Nanny Nan looked back toward the dining room and said, "Oh, for goodness' sake. You! Dog! Get down!" She left the hallway and returned to the dining room, where, we can only assume, Cassie had jumped onto John's chair and was eating his meatloaf.

Professor Templeton looked up at Dean D. Dean with a completely baffled expression and indicated the notebook. "This is utter gibberish," he said. "It makes no sense whatsoever. Unless . . ." He handed the notebook to Abigail. "Can you read any of this, Abby?"

As I know you know, Abigail was the word puzzle expert of the family. Do you have a word puzzle expert in your family? Well, too bad. It so happens that I *do,* and that that expert—you will hardly be surprised to learn—is me. **LET'S MOVE ON**.

Abigail examined the notebook. Dean D. Dean sidled over beside her, pointed at a particular passage, and said in a triumphant way, "There. See?!"

This is what it said: "helcpt prsnl trans. Indiv unit napsk."

"I think it says, 'helicopter personal transportation,'" Abigail said.

"And 'individual unit knapsack.'"

**AHA!** cried Dean D. Dean.

"There's no 'aha,'" John said. "The only reason you wrote 'knapsack' was because our father probably said it in his lecture."

"There *is* an 'aha'!"

"No, there's not."

"I say 'aha'!"

"It doesn't matter what you say. There's no 'aha.'"

**AHA AHA AHA AHA!**

"Nope. Sorry."

Dean D. Dean snatched the notebook back from Abigail and glared at the Professor. "You don't understand," he said, no longer trying to sound happy or friendly. "This is your last chance."

"Absolute rubbish," the Professor said. "Last chance before what?"

"Before . . ." Dean D. Dean nodded solemnly. "Before certain *things* take place."

"Mr. Dean, we have indulged you quite enough," the Professor said. "Now take your notebook and your certain things and kindly leave our home before I summon the authorities."

Dean D. Dean drew himself up until he was standing as tall as he could, tugged his elegant suit jacket down with a snap, and gave his tie knot a little squeeze.

He looked at the twins. "I wish you twins had never been born," he said. "And I'm not just saying that. I really do!"

He marched off the porch and down the walk and off into the night. John shut the door behind him. Then the twins and their father went back into the dining room to see what kind of trouble Cassie had gotten into.

## QUESTIONS FOR REVIEW

1. How would the Templeton twins' lives have been different had they never been born?

2. Do you have a recipe for meatloaf you would care to share with the Narrator?*

3. Multiple choice (circle one): When Dean D. Dean says, "Before certain *things* take place," what does he mean?

   a. Don't know.   c. Beats me.   e. All of the above.
   b. No idea.      d. Not a clue.

*Probably you do not. Therefore I shall share one with you, so the next time someone asks you for a meatloaf recipe you will be prepared. It is a recipe for something I call:

# THE NARRATOR'S MEATLOAF

## *You will need:*

**1 grown-up** (This can be a parent, neighbor, long-lost uncle or aunt, piano teacher, or any other convenient adult.)

**1 tablespoon vegetable oil** (You know, of course, that vegetable oil is not something used to oil rusty vegetables. It is oil extracted from corn, peanuts, safflowers, soybeans, or whatever.)

**1/2 cup chopped onions** (Do not attempt to chop the onions yourself. Kitchen knives are sharp, and onions are frisky and hard to corral. Ask your grown-up to chop the onions.)

**1 or 2 cloves garlic, pressed** (This does not mean you should send the garlic cloves to the dry cleaner's and have them pressed and hung on a hanger. It means you should put them through a garlic press. You can do this yourself.)

**1/2 tablespoon cumin** (This is a spice that is used in all the most delicious foods in the world, so don't be afraid of it.)

**1 teaspoon oregano** (This is often put on pizza, so it may look familiar. If you want to impress your grown-up, crush it in your fingers before you add it. When someone remarks about it, just say, "Oh, yes, I always crush my dried herbs. Otherwise, what's the point?")

**1/2 cup ketchup** (You know what this is, surely.)

**1 pound ground beef** (You may find it icky and unpleasant to work with raw ground beef, but how else do you think meatloaf is made? Oh, never mind. Ask your grown-up to help you with this.)

**1 egg, lightly beaten** (This does not mean you should take a whip or a club and "beat" the egg. It means you should break it and stir it up in a cup with a fork so that the clear and the yellow parts mix together. Yes, a raw egg. Oh, please, it's just an egg. Don't be so squeamish. But be sure to wash your hands if you get any on them, and to wipe off the counter if any spills.)

**1 cup (more or less) breadcrumbs** (These are not literally crumbs that fall off bread, but breadcrumbs that come in a tall, round can.)

**Salt and pepper** (These are self-explanatory.)

# You Should Do This:

1. Instruct your grown-up to preheat the oven to 350 degrees. FAHRENHEIT (or 177 degrees Celsius). Preheating the oven to 350 degrees Celsius (= 662 degrees Fahrenheit) would destroy the oven and burn down the house. This is highly undesirable and will result in no meatloaf.

2. Using your grown-up with great care and politeness, do the following three things:

   a. Put a pan on the stove and turn the heat to medium. Add the oil. After about 30 seconds, add the onions and cook, stirring, until they get glassy-looking and you can sort of see through them.

   b. Lower the heat a little, add the garlic, and cook for half a minute, stirring. Don't let it burn or even get brown.

   c. Add the cumin, oregano, and ketchup. *Yes, you are COOKING the ketchup.* Cook, stirring, for 15 seconds. Then turn off the heat and let this mixture cool. Go do something else for 10 minutes or until the mixture really is cool to the touch.

3. Put the ground beef in a big bowl. Add the beaten egg, the breadcrumbs, and the onion-ketchup mixture. Add a couple pinches of salt and a couple shakes of pepper.

4. Combine all of this with your bare hands, smushing it together gently, but be sure the ingredients are thoroughly mixed. You heard me: WITH YOUR BARE HANDS. You are probably thinking, "But surely there is some other way!" No. There is no other way.

5. Dump it all out onto a roasting pan (one that has raised edges all around, not a flat cookie sheet) and form it into a "loaf" about the size and shape of a cigar box. Be sure it's fairly even and flat across the top and that there is space between the loaf and pan edge on all four sides. If you want, you can dribble some more ketchup all over the top.

6. Utilize your grown-up to do the following two things:

   a. Put the pan in the oven and bake for 45 minutes.

   b. Remove from oven, let cool slightly, then cut and serve.

You may add more ketchup at the table, and don't let anyone tell you otherwise. After all, you're (with the help of your grown-up) the cook! (Remember to turn the oven off and to thank your grown-up profusely for all of his or her help. If necessary, look up "profusely" in the dictionary.)

# CHAPTER 9

# MORE (IF YOU CAN BELIEVE IT) EXCITING THINGS START TO HAPPEN

The next day the twins were home alone with Nanny Nan. It was just before lunchtime. John and Abigail were in the dining room, looking through a big book of maps that was so gigantic they had to put it on the dining table. They had just finished examining the map of France and turned to the map of Spain. Cassie was sleeping under the dining room table. The doorbell rang.

Cassie immediately woke up, started barking, and ran toward the front door. The twins were eager to see who could be visiting them so soon after the move into their new home. But Nanny Nan got there first. They heard the door open and Nanny Nan say, "Yes?"

Cassie was barking too much for them to hear what the visitor said. Finally Nanny Nan called out, "Children, please collect this creature and take her elsewhere!" So Abigail dashed to the front door and picked up Cassie. She tried to see who was at the door, but Nanny Nan was blocking the way. Abigail carried Cassie back to the living room, where John was waiting.

Then a slightly familiar voice said, very smoothly and pleasantly, "Hello. I've been sent by Professor

Elton Templeton for the children. The Professor thinks it would a fine idea if they went on a little outing with me."

The twins waited and listened. Cassie squirmed around in Abigail's arms in a ridiculous fashion.

"An outing?" Nanny Nan said. "What kind of outing?"

"Oh, you know," the man said. "A ride in the country. A pleasant excursion into the surrounding landscape."

"The Professor didn't tell me anything about any 'outing,'" the nanny said.

"Of course not, Madame," the voice said. "We only just discussed it mere moments ago. The Professor and I myself. Professor Templeton. Professor Elton Templeton. The father of the lovely children in question. The famous *inventor*."

"Oh, baloney," the nanny said. "First of all, you speak in a weird manner. Second, if the Professor wants the children to go on an outing, have him call me and tell me so himself."

"Madame," the man said. "I can assure you—"

"You can't assure me of anything," Nanny Nan said. "I can assure *you* that either you get lost or I'm going

to call the police." And with that Nanny Nan firmly and loudly shut the door.

"Who was that, Nanny Nan?" Abigail called out, putting Cassie back on the floor.

"No one," the nanny said. "Just a man with a silly moustache."

After lunch the twins were each in their rooms, pursuing their hobbies. John was practicing with his drumsticks on a practice pad (because Nanny Nan still would not let him play the drums themselves). Meanwhile, Abigail had persuaded Nanny Nan to let her work on her cryptic puzzles for one hour, as long as she read the clues out loud. She had just read this clue and was thinking about it:

*Red treat found in burlap pleasantly (5).*

(Here is another hint about solving cryptics: Some clues hide the answer right in front of you, and you don't even have to unscramble any letters. When you see clues like "found in" or "hidden in," it's a signal to look at the arrangement of the letters in the clue itself. Sometimes the answer is formed by combining the letters that end one word with the letters that begin the next word. Is that the case here?)

Abigail—

(Wait. Another tip for doing cryptics: Look for unusual words. Those are quite often the words that contain the letters necessary for the answer. Do you see an unusual word? Oh, please. You do so. I think we can all agree that "burlap" is an unusual word.

Can I assume you know what it is? Very well: Burlap is a kind of rough, scratchy woven material used in bags that hold things like potatoes—and like the onions you yourself may have used when you made the meatloaf in the previous chapter. You did make the meatloaf, didn't you? Wasn't it delicious? You can thank me later.)

Abigail studied the word "burlap." Was the answer to be found in its first two or three letters, combined with letters from the word before it? But no—"inbur" was not a word.

And then she saw the answer: a five-letter word using the *last* two letters of "burlap" and the first three letters of "pleasantly."

Which is indeed a red treat.

THE TEMPLETON TWINS HAVE AN IDEA

Feeling very happy and satisfied, she had just finished writing the answer in the box when she heard an unfamiliar voice, right behind her, say very quietly, "Turn around and don't say anything."

She turned around and didn't say anything. Standing there was a man who looked—well, not like someone she knew, but *like* someone who *looked like* someone she knew. He was wearing blue jeans and a white shirt and a light beige windbreaker—*not* a beautiful, wonderful suit and tie.

"How did you get in here?" Abigail asked.

"I walked in through the front door," the man said.

"And Cassie didn't bark at you?"

"Who? The dog? She's asleep on the couch."

So there you have it: The one time it would have been helpful for Cassie to bark, no matter how ridiculously, at someone coming into the house, she was asleep. I hardly know what to say about such a thing.

"Call your brother," the man said in a whisper.

"What? I can't hear you," Abigail said.

"I said, call your brother," he whispered a bit more loudly.

"Why should I?" Abigail said. "Who are you? What are you doing here?"

The man said softly, "Here's why you should," and from his pocket he pulled out an actual gun.

Abigail's heart thumped one hard thump. "John?" she called. "Can you come here for a second?"

The man stood off to the side as John appeared in the doorway. He took one look at his sister and stopped dead. He knew something was wrong.

The man pulled John into the room, shut the door behind him, and pointed the gun at both the Templeton twins. "Now you kids are going to be very, very quiet," he said in a whisper. "We're going to go down the steps and out the door and into my car. Period. End of discussion."

"We haven't had a discussion," Abigail pointed out.

"Just . . . quiet. No talking. Period."

"You look familiar," John said. "I mean, sort of."

"I said, no talking," the man said very, very quietly. "Now everyone is just going to just calm down."

"We are calm," John said.

"Calm and *quiet*." The man gestured toward the door with the gun. "Now, very, very quietly, now, we're—"

The door flew open with a bang. **"IT'S TOO QUIET IN HERE,"** Nanny Nan said. "I think you two are trying to *get away* with . . ." Then she saw the man, and the gun, and stopped talking.

"They're coming with me," the man said.

"Children," Nanny Nan said. "Do what he says." Then she said to the man, "Just don't harm them."

"No one is going to be harmed if they do what I say," the man said.

"Then put the gun away," Nanny Nan said.

"They have to do what I say first."

"They will. Just put the gun away."

"Why don't you give the gun to me?" John said.

The man made a face. "That's not how it works."

"We won't harm you," Abigail said. "Just give John the gun and we'll do what you say."

"Right," John said. "We promise we won't harm you."

"No, *I* promise I won't harm *you*," the man said. "But first y—"

Everyone stopped as they heard a loud noise from downstairs. It sounded like someone slamming the front door. Then they listened as a man angrily stomped up the

stairs, muttering to himself. A moment later this person appeared in the doorway. He looked like Dean D. Dean would look were he wearing a big fake moustache, since that is indeed who he was and what he was wearing. "Can we please move this along?" he said to the first man.

The Templeton twins stared at the man who had just arrived. "It's you," John said. "Why are you wearing a fake moustache?"

"This is a real moustache, little boy," the man said. "And I've never seen you before in my life."

"Yes, you have," Abigail said. "You're Dean D. Dean."

I MOST CERTAINLY AM NOT.  YES, YOU ARE.

AM NOT.  ARE.

A.

AM NOT.  ARE SO.

"OH, ALL RIGHT! YES! I AM!" Dean D. Dean tore off the big fake moustache and threw it on the floor. "Now let's go."

"I knew I should have called the police," Nanny Nan said. "Outing. Baloney!"

"What does the 'D' stand for?" Abigail asked.

"It—never mind what the 'D' stands for. You're coming with us."

"Does it stand for Dean?" Abigail asked.

"No!" Dean D. Dean said.

"The 'D' in *my* name stands for Dean," the first man said.

"Who are you?" John asked.

Dean D. Dean went over to the first man, ripped the gun out of his hand, and pointed it at the twins. "He's my brother."

"I'm Dan D. Dean," the brother said.

"Hey!" John said. "You're twins!"

It was true. Dean and Dan Dean were, in fact, identical twins, which means they looked almost exactly alike. The Templeton twins were not only one boy and one girl, but they looked just slightly alike. They were what is called "fraternal" twins.

You will have realized by now that Dan D. Dean was also a handsome man, since he was the identical twin of Dean D. Dean, who was himself, as I have made abundantly clear, a handsome man. Of course, because identical twins are not always entirely identical, it was possible

that Dan wasn't quite as handsome as Dean. And, indeed, this was the case.

"Yes, yes, all right, we're twins," Dean D. Dean said. He pointed the gun at Nanny Nan and gestured toward the door. "Now let's go." Then he turned to his brother and said, "Bring them."

Nanny Nan walked out of the room with Dean D. Dean holding the gun behind her. They went downstairs.

"Why are you doing this?" John asked Dan D. Dean.

"Because your father stole Dean's idea thirteen years ago," Dan said. "And that's not right!"

"It's also not true," Abigail said. "Our father has plenty of ideas of his own. He doesn't need to steal anyone else's idea."

"That's not what Dean says," Dan said.

"He's lying!" John said.

"DAN!" Dean shouted from downstairs. "I'm WAITING."

That was enough, finally, to wake up Cassie. She started barking.

Abigail and John traded a look that said, wordlessly, "Let's go. Perhaps, with the distraction provided by the barking Cassie, we will be able to think of some way to improve our situation by the time we get downstairs." They slowly filed out of the room toward the stairs, with Dan D. Dean behind them.

Then, from the kitchen downstairs, they heard Dean D. Dean yell, "Put that phone down!"

"I will not!" they heard Nanny Nan say. "Hello? Police?"

"I said, put it down!"

"What do you mean, wrong number? I'm calling the police!"

"Lady, I'm going to count to three—"

"Oh, be quiet. I'm on the phone."

"One . . . two . . ."

"Hello? Police?"

**BANG!** And then **CRASH!** Or, actually, the sound was more like two sounds in one: **BANG–CRASH!**

The twins, nearing the bottom of the stairs, both jerked in surprise. The sound was loud and sudden and echoed throughout the house. Then, to their amazement, they heard Dean D. Dean say, **"OW!"**

The twins ran into the kitchen. There they saw Dean D. Dean rubbing his right elbow with his left hand.

His right hand still held the gun. Behind him a little window in the door to the pantry had shattered. Broken glass was everywhere—and Nanny Nan lay on the floor, her eyes closed. Cassie stood nearby, barking, as if that helped matters, which it did not.

Dean D. Dean seized Abigail by her arm and started dragging her toward the front door. "Let's go."

"But what about Nanny Nan?" Abigail cried.

"Leave her. She's dead."

"What?" Abigail said. "Are you sure?"

"Yes, I'm sure. Now move."

"Then why isn't she bleeding?"

"She had a heart attack!"

John started toward the phone mounted on the kitchen wall. "Then we have to call an ambulance."

Dean D. Dean rudely shoved Abigail toward her brother and held up the gun. "Do you want me to shoot her? Let's go."

John froze. He thought for a second. Finally he lowered his hand from the phone and said, "Okay. But we have to bring Cassie."

Dan D. Dean said, "Actually, Dean, if we bring the dog—"

"OUT OF THE QUESTION!"

"But they might cooperate more if we let them."

"We are not going on a picnic!" Dean D. Dean yelled. "We are acquiring two hostages!"

"Please?" Abigail said.

"Absolutely not!"

"Then we're not coming," John said. He turned to Abigail and said, "I'm going upstairs to play the drums. What are you going to do?"

"OH, ALL RIGHT!" Dean D. Dean yelled. "BRING THE STUPID DOG!"

He waited, gnashing his perfect white teeth, while Cassie jumped up and down three hundred and seventy-one times before Abigail got the leash on her. Then Dean D. Dean said, "Finally. All right. Everybody. MOVE."

In the front of the house was a black SUV with its motor running. Yes, they had left the motor running all this time, filling the air with exhaust and wasting fuel. *That's* how bad they were.

Dan D. Dean opened the rear door, and Cassie jumped in as though everyone were going on a fun trip. Then Dean D. Dean flung Abigail and John into the back and got into the driver's seat as Dan got into the passenger's seat. Dean D. Dean threw the SUV into gear and sped off with the Templeton twins (and their ridiculous dog) as his prisoners.

## QUESTIONS FOR REVIEW

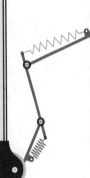

1. Can you spell *moustache*?*

2. Solve this cryptic clue, if you aren't too terribly busy: *There's a bad man in Wade and D. E. Anderson (4,1,4)***

3. Isn't this exciting?
   a. Yes, very.
   b. Yes, exceedingly.
   c. I cannot even answer this question, I am in such an advanced state of excitement.

---

* You can now. Moustache is a French word. Other French words you may find your-self using in daily life include French toast, French fries, and French-cut green beans.

** I refuse to tell you the answer to this. It's too easy as it is. I will not even give you a hint. Just ignore the punctuation mark in the clue. All right, I see I have indeed just given you a hint. But that's all. You're on your own from here on out.

# CHAPTER 10

# DOWN IN THE DISMAL, DANK, AND DREARY DUNGEON OF DEAN D. AND DAN D. DEAN*

---

*I invite you to say this ten times very fast. Or even moderately fast. The important thing is that you say it ten times. Ready? Begin.

D ean D. Dean and Dan D. Dean and the Templeton twins drove for about half an hour. During the drive, the Ridiculous Dog, of course, wanted to jump onto the driver's lap, which is how she always liked to ride in a car, with her pointy nose out the window or, in an even more ridiculous fashion, rubbing against the glass and creating a lot of silly marks while she gazed with wild excitement at perfectly ordinary sights. But John kept hold of her leash and made her stay in the back.

Finally they reached a house out in the country, at the end of a dirt road, far from the main highway and even farther from any other houses or people. It was a big, old two-story house made of faded white wood planks that were warped and splintery and peeling from age and poor upkeep. Around the yard were old pieces of lawn furniture, a rusted-out lawn mower, and not a bit of lawn.

"You two are going to be in big trouble," John said. "Nanny Nan called the police. They're going to find you guys and throw you in jail."

"It's called kidnapping," Abigail said. "It's a very serious crime."

"Shut *up*," Dean D. Dean said. "First, Nanny Nan got a wrong number. And then she died. And that wasn't my fault! Because I missed. She had a heart attack."

"That's attempted murder!" John said.

"Son," Dean D. Dean said, "Believe me, there w—"

"I'm not your son."

"I KNOW YOU'RE NOT MY SON. JUST SHUT UP AND LISTEN. Young man, there will be no police. But do not fret. As soon as your father comes through, I'll let you go."

"What do you mean, 'comes through'?" Abigail asked.

"Simple." Dean D. Dean stopped the black SUV on a gravel-covered area in front of the house, next to an old car painted a tired metallic blue. He switched off the engine, then turned around and looked at the twins. "Your father," he said, "has to acknowledge to the world that the Personal One-Man Helicopter that you put in a knapsack was my idea—"

"But it wasn't just *your* idea," Abigail said. "Everybody has had that idea."

"I had that idea when I was four," John said. "And Papa had already been working on it by then."

"—and he has to turn over to me all the titles and patents and ownership of said helicopter, both legal and moral and financial, in all media known and to be invented, both foreign and domestic, now and in the future, in real time and in perpetuity, throughout the universe, from here to eternity, henceforth and forevermore, as long as we both shall live."

"Amen," said Dan D. Dean.

The brothers got out of the car. Each opened a rear door and each took a twin roughly by the arm. Abigail held onto Cassie's leash, and the frisky, bright white dog jumped out, too.

The Dean brothers dragged the Templeton twins into the poorly kept house. It smelled of fried salami, beer, and insecticide, although probably the twins couldn't really identify the smells. They did know, however, that it smelled bad.

"This way," Dean D. Dean said, and shoved the twins into the kitchen. Abigail noticed what appeared to be a simple drawing of a balloon in a box mounted with magnets on the light green refrigerator.

But before she could examine it, Dean D. Dean banged open a door and propelled her and John through it and down a wobbly wooden staircase into the basement.

The basement was lit by three harsh, glaring, bare lightbulbs and a bit of daylight coming in through four dirty, screened-over windows high on the walls. The room smelled like moist earth, which wasn't so bad. But it was damp and uncomfortable. It felt like a room where bugs should be and people should not be. Cassie, of course, wagged her tail rapidly and looked perky and ready for anything, as though this were just the next thrilling episode in a glorious adventure.

"You two make yourselves comfortable," Dean D. Dean said. "I will contact your father and tell him the terms of your release."

"Wait a minute," John said. "The Personal One-Man Helicopter isn't even finished yet. Papa says he has a—" He turned to his sister. "What's it called?"

"A prototype," she said.

"Yeah. A prototype. But that's all. He hasn't sold it to any company yet. So there's no money. You're going to tell him to give you stuff that he doesn't even have!"

Dean D. Dean smiled.

While he is smiling, let me tell you what a "proto-type" is. Unless, of course, you already know. Do you? Oh, you do? Isn't that splendid? Good for you. Then why don't you tell me what it is? Go on. I'm waiting.

I notice you haven't told me anything. Very well, then, I shall tell *you*. When you invent a new thing, you make a sample of it to show to other people, to demon-strate what it does and how it works. It's your specially handmade, original first example of an invention. There are usually only a few prototypes of a new invention, and often there is only one.

Don't even bother telling me you already knew that, because I simply won't believe you.

Dean D. Dean stopped smiling. "It's not just about the money," he said. "I want the recognition. I want to be known far and wide as the man who invented the Per-sonal One-Man Helicopter that you put in a knapsack. People will look at me and think, 'Hey, wait a minute— HE invented that helicopter? Good for him!' Then a col-lege will give me an honorary degree. Then a university will hire me to be dean of the college of arts and sciences."

Abigail said, "But that would make you Dean Dean D. Dean."

"Exactly!" the man said with a wild, crazed smile.

"Dean Dean D. Dean?" Abigail said. "It sounds silly."

"It sounds like 'Here Comes the Bride,'" John said.

Dean D. Dean looked angry. "Just wait here," he snarled. "And don't try screaming for help. There's nobody within twenty miles of this place."

And with that he stomped up the old wooden stairs and slammed the door behind him.

John sighed. Then he walked quietly up the stairs and slowly tried the doorknob. It turned, but when he pushed against the door, it didn't move. He went back down the steps. "It's locked," he told Abigail.

"Maybe there's another door somewhere," she said.

As the twins wandered around looking for another door, they were able to see exactly what was in the basement.

There was a lot.

There were old wooden tables and old wooden chairs, and old cans spattered with leftover paint along with paintbrushes that had turned crusty and hard. There were piles of lumber. Standing in the middle of everything, like a giant hulking beast, was a huge, round black furnace, with monstrous arms snaking out of it in different directions and disappearing into the ceiling. There was a stack of mirrors leaning against a wall, some with frames and some without. There were a million cardboard boxes full of stuff. There were old ladders, old lamps, old ropes, random piles of bricks and rocks, and a dust-covered bag of cement. There was a huge, rusty old wrench that weighed a ton. Oh, yes—there were spider-webs everywhere, too.

What there wasn't was another door.

"You know," Abigail said. "Just because Dean D. Dean said that there weren't any people nearby if we called for help, doesn't mean it's true."

John nodded. The twins each took a deep breath and began to yell for help.

Now, I don't know if you've ever had the experience of yelling for help. It is pretty much a straightforward matter of shouting, "Help!" as loudly as you can. And

that is what the twins did. Cassie, of course, thought this activity was for her benefit, so—quite ridiculously—she began barking back at the twins.

This went on for about two minutes, which isn't a very long time when it comes to such matters as cooking dinner or flying to Brazil, but when it involves continual shouting as hard as you can it is a fairly long time. And finally it brought results.

Unfortunately for the twins, the results were not as they had hoped. No one came to help them. Instead, the door at the top of the stairs opened and Dan D. Dean came halfway down the steps. "You're wasting your breath," he said. "There's no one within fifty miles of this place."

"Your brother said twenty miles," John said.

"Fine. Twenty. Just stop. Besides," he added, "Dean just left to pick up your father. Once he gives Dean everything connected with the Personal One-Man Helicopter, we'll let you go." Dan D. Dean started to go back up the stairs.

"Wait!" Abigail said. "Why are you doing this? We know why your brother is, because he's crazy. But why are you?"

Dan D. Dean looked at her as though she had asked the silliest question in the world. "I have to," he said. "We're twins." And with that Dan D. Dean went back up the steps and shut the door again.

"That's ridiculous," John said. "I don't do something just because you do it."

His sister nodded a little, as though she were thinking of something else. Which, John knew, she was. Suddenly she looked at him and said, "This is serious. We have to get out of here."

"Because Papa won't give Dean D. Dean the helicopter?"

She shook her head. "No. Because even if Papa does give him everything he asked for, they're not going to let us go. They've kidnapped us! If they let us go, we'll tell the police and they'll go to jail."

John felt his mouth go dry, which is what happens when you become really, really afraid of something. "You're right. Dean D. Dean killed Nanny Nan—"

"—which means he'll try to kill us, too."

## QUESTIONS FOR REVIEW

1. What is burlap? Do you think it is anything different now than it was in the previous chapter?

2. Check one: The Narrator's definition of "prototype" was interesting and complete.

   Yes ☐                    Yes, very ☐

3. Match the items in Column A with the descriptions in Column B:

   | Column A | Column B |
   | --- | --- |
   | a. This chapter | a. Excellent |
   | b. The last chapter | b. Fascinating |
   | c. The next chapter | c. Perfect |
   | d. The Narrator | d. Wonderful |

THE TEMPLETON TWINS HAVE AN IDEA

# CHAPTER 11

# OTHER THINGS HAPPEN IN AN EXCITING MANNER!

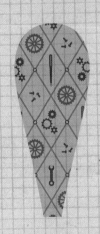

**Y**ou will remember that earlier I said that the Templeton twins' hobbies would prove to be extremely important later in the story. If you don't remember me saying that, I urge you to turn back to Chapter 2 (the first Chapter 2) and refresh your memory, because I distinctly remember saying it, and I remember you reading it.

And now is when the twins' hobbies will prove to be very important. So pay close attention, because I almost hear you thinking, "How can doing crossword puzzles or playing the drums *possibly* help the twins get out of the Deans' horrible basement?" And now I am going to tell you.

After Abigail delivered to her brother the rather upsetting observation that Dean D. Dean probably wanted to kill them, John said, "We have to escape. Maybe we can break our way out of here."

He looked around until he saw an old, folded-up ladder lying on the floor. He dragged it over to one of the windows, opened it up, and braced it against the wall. Yes, this kicked up a lot of dust and dirt and was extremely unpleasant, but what do you expect? He worked his way up the ladder to the window and examined it.

Then he said, "Oh, nuts," and climbed back down. He went over to his sister and said, "The windows have bars across them on the outside."

Abigail looked around the dank, dirty basement and up the wobbly stairs to the locked door and said, "So we can't escape."

"Thanks a lot," John said, in what I'm sure we can all agree was a sarcastic tone of voice.

Abigail shook her head. "I don't mean, let's give up. I just mean that we can't escape in that . . . *escape-y* way of breaking out of here." Abigail, of course, knew better than almost anyone that the words you use to think about something can determine how much success you have in dealing with it. "If we think about *escaping,* we'll never get anywhere because we can't do it ourselves. So let's not think about escaping."

"Then what should we think about?!" John protested.

"Let's think about *leaving,*" Abigail said. "What we need to think about is how we can leave."

John said, "Oh." He thought for a second. "Well, we can leave if someone lets us leave."

"Okay, so who can let us leave?"

John said, "There's only one person. Dan D. Dean."

"Right. And what do we need him to do?"

John shrugged. "Open the door. And then get out of the way."

"So how do we get him to do that?"

They discussed it. Getting Dan D. Dean to open the basement door didn't seem too difficult. On the other hand, convincing him to get out of the way did seem like a hard problem to solve.

John said, "We can't just *ask* him to get out of the way. Because he'll say no."

Then Abigail said, "It would work if we could just keep him from being *in* the way."

John nodded. He looked around the dirty, cluttered, dank basement. "Suppose we get Dan D. Dean to open the door and come down here," he said. "What would surprise him? What's the last thing you expect to see when you come into a room?"

Abigail thought for a second, then smiled. She told John her idea. He said, "Yes!" And then he got busy.

Now, one thing you learn about when you play the drums is *equipment*. Why? Because a set of drums consists of a lot of things that have to be mounted and hooked up to one another. If you take the set to play at a party or a concert, you have to take it all apart and then mount and hook up everything again. And then take it all apart to bring it home and then put it all together *again*. It's the only instrument I know of that you have to rebuild every time you move it.

Thus, when you play the drums, you learn about *stuff*.

You learn about drumheads made of plastic and hoops, and wooden shells and metal lugs and nuts and bolts and stands and keys and clamps. You learn about little pads made of felt and little pieces of plastic tubing. You learn about springs and footplates and tension rods. You get a lot of experience in attaching and clamping and tightening and loosening and things like that.

So John surveyed the basement to see what kind of *equipment* the twins had at their disposal. As I have already taken the trouble to inform you, there was a great deal. The question was, how could they use it to achieve their goal? John said that they could maybe do this, or that, or some other thing. Then John suggested a certain idea, and Abigail said it was perfect.

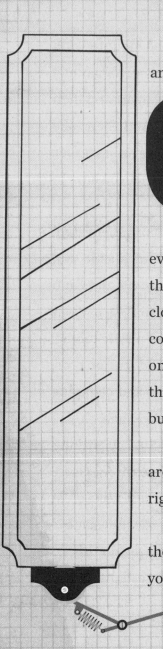

At which point, of course, John said—and you may say it with me now—

## LET'S DO IT AND VIEW IT!

Yes, all of this is very exciting. However, it is my duty to inform you that, as they enacted their plan, they got their clothes dirty. They got grime and dust and cobwebs and various kinds of icky things on their formerly clean clothes. I know this upsets you as much as it upsets me, but we must all just learn to live with it.

The first thing they did was to look around the dirty basement for just the right kind of mirror. And they found it.

This mirror was tall and narrow, of the kind that you hang on a closet door so you can see your entire body when you're

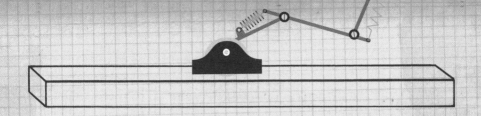

trying on clothes to go to the ball, or the show, or the dance, or the prom, or wherever it is people like you go when you get dressed up. It was, of course, dirty and scratched and not very attractive for use in your bedroom, but it would do.

Next they looked around for and found some thin rope. Then they needed something that would hang on the rope without falling off—and they found it when they discovered an ancient tool-box that contained a bunch of S-hooks. These are hooks in the form of the letter "S," which, as you are no doubt aware, is shaped like this: S.

They hunted around among the old lamps until they found one that still worked. Then John climbed up the ladder, wrapped an old cloth around his hand, and used it to unscrew one of the hot bulbs shining in the ceiling light socket.

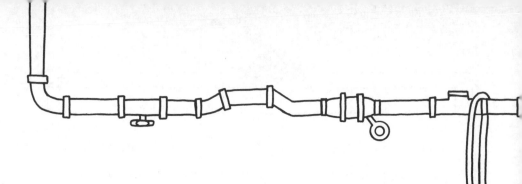

Then came the hard part: They moved the ladder to a particular place. They tied the ends of the thin rope together, forming a big loop. Then John climbed up the ladder and hung the big loop of rope over a pipe running across the ceiling. It was like draping a rubber band over a pencil. They ended up with two smile-shaped loops of rope hanging down from the pipe, *which hung above the lowest step on the stairway.*

I wrote that in italics because it's important. You'll see why if you keep reading, which, of course, you will.

Then they brought the two hanging smile-shaped loops of rope together and hung two S-hooks from the ropes. And then, holding their breath in suspense, they hung the mirror. They did this by jamming the free ends of the two S-hooks underneath the top of the mirror's frame (at the back), so that the whole mirror dangled freely off the hooks.

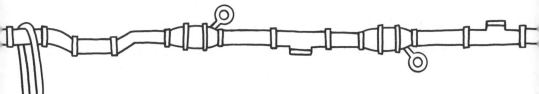

You may be thinking, "Hey—hanging the mirror off those S-hooks is sort of like when they hung the dog's picture off the fishhook!" I would tip my hat to you if you thought that—and if I actually wore a hat, and if you actually thought it.

The mirror was now hanging off the rope, hovering over the last step of the stairway. The mirror's frame didn't break because the mirror was pretty light.

Then they put the bulb that John had removed from its socket into the old lamp they had chosen, and found an outlet on the ceiling, and plugged it in. (Yes, there were outlets on the ceiling. Old basements have these all the time, so you will simply have to accept it.) The outlet worked. The lamp worked. So they tied some rope to the lamp and hung that from another pipe on the ceiling.

I know you are exhausted from following this description of what the Templeton twins did. I am, too. But it will all pay off soon, so please continue reading as I continue writing.

The twins now had the mirror hanging straight down at the foot of the steps, and the lighted lamp hanging farther up the steps. John looked around until he found a solid piece of lumber that wasn't too long or heavy. He picked up Cassie's leash and wrapped its loop end around his hand a couple times so he had it good and tight.

Abigail dug a hammer out of the old toolbox. She walked up the steps and, as she expected, found the light switch for the entire basement near the door.

She turned off the lights. Luckily it was daytime, so—even though the basement was fairly gloomy and dark—enough light came from the windows that she could come partially back down the steps without difficulty.

They were ready.

Abigail said, "Okay. Let's do it." Then, as loudly as she could, she started yelling, **"OW! OW!** It hurts! **OW!"**

John started yelling, "Help! Dan! Abigail is hurt!

It didn't take long for the twins to hear hasty, pounding footsteps in the kitchen above. The basement door swung open, and Dan D. Dean appeared at the top of the steps.

# IT WAS THEN THAT THE FOLLOWING EXCITING THINGS HAPPENED, IN THIS ORDER:

**1** Dan D. Dean squinted into the basement and noticed that **the lights were out.** He turned them on with the switch at the top of the stairs.

**2** When the lights came on, the lamp that the Templeton twins had hung shined right in his face.

**2A** Cassie, the R. Dog, barked ridiculously.

BARK BARK BARK

BARK BARK BARK

BARK BARK BARK

**3** Dan D. Dean took a step or two down the stairs and saw something that so startled and disturbed him that he **yelled,**

**HAA!**

**4** At that moment, Abigail availed herself of the opportunity to **smash** him in the foot with the hammer.

**YAAHH!**

**5** He **stumbled** down the steps and **crashed** into the hanging mirror.

**5A** Cassie, the R. D., barked in an r. manner.

RRRRRRRRRRRRRRRRRRRRRRR

**6** John elected at that moment to **whack** Dan D. Dean across the legs with the piece of lumber.

**AAHH!**

**7** Dan D. Dean fell forward, grabbing the mirror for support.

**8** The mirror came off its S-hooks and, it goes almost without saying, went **crashing** onto the floor along with Dan D. Dean.

**8A** Cassie barked uselessly.

BARKETY BARK BARK BARK

BARK

BARK BARK BARK

BARK BARK BARK BARK BARK BARK

**9** The Templeton twins (John dragging Cassie) ran up the steps into the kitchen, shut the basement door, and locked it.

**10** THEY RAN OUTSIDE.

Cassie looked around in the sunshine at the trees and the tired old lawn furniture and the general array of yard junk, her mouth open and her pink tongue gently bobbing up and down as she panted with excitement, then looked up at the twins with bright eyes and an expression that said,

THAT WAS FUN! THIS IS GREAT! WHAT'S NEXT?

(No, wait. First, when they were running through the kitchen, Abigail's eyes fell on that drawing of a balloon mounted on the refrigerator. By that, I do not mean that her eyeballs literally dropped out of her head onto the drawing. I mean the picture caught her attention.)

*Then* they ran outside. And that's when things got really tricky.

## QUESTIONS FOR REVIEW

1. What is the difference between escaping and leaving? Write your answer in the form of a poem here:

2. What is the difference between "HAA!" and "YAAHH!"? Be specific.

3. What is the difference between being hit in the foot with a hammer and being whacked in the legs with a piece of wood? Draw a beautiful picture illustrating your answer.

CHAPTER 12

# THE TEMPLETON TWINS THINK OF SOMETHING THAT EVEN THE NARRATOR HAS TO ADMIT IS CLEVER

**S**o there they were: out of the basement and outside.

Because, you see, when John asked, "What's the last thing you expect to see when you come into a room?" Abigail had answered, "Yourself."

And how true that is—not only for me (the Narrator) and for you (the Reader), but for Dan D. Dean. Even if you're a twin, you don't expect to see *yourself* when you walk into a room, or down a set of steps into a basement. So when Dan D. Dean saw himself (in the well-positioned mirror, nicely illuminated by the hanging lamp), he was completely stunned.

Very clever, Templeton twins.

Now they were outside—and free! Free!

*Or were they?*

(When someone—a Narrator, for example—says something, and then immediately asks, in italics, if it's really true, you can be pretty sure that the answer is no, it's not really true. And indeed, this was the case with the Templeton twins.)

They were "free" because they had gotten out of the Dean brothers' basement. But they (and their you-know-what dog) were also in the middle of nowhere, maybe dozens of miles from their home or the police or anyone who could help them, and they had nothing to help themselves. So they weren't really "free." They were just outside.

From the house they heard a muffled BANG and then "OW!" This was the sound of Dan D. Dean slamming himself into the basement door and trying to break the lock. It was a pretty strong lock, and he wasn't getting very far.

"We have to get home and help Papa!" John said. "Or—no. Wait. He's probably at the lab. Come on."

You will recall, I am sure, that earlier I made mention of an old metallic blue car in the front yard of the poorly kept house. I say "I am sure" because I assume you are an intelligent and attentive reader. (This is only fitting, as I am an intelligent and attentive writer.) Please do everything you can (which means reading intelligently and attentively) not to disappoint me in this regard. Although I see we are on page 160, so it's a little late in the day for me to ask this. All right, then, begin reading intelligently and attentively *now*.

There was an old metallic blue car in the front yard. It was one of those long, low, wide American models from many years ago. You may be thinking, "Hey! Maybe the key is in the car! That always happens in the movies! People who have to get away jump into a strange car, and the key just happens to be in it!"

Yes, this kind of thing does happen in the movies. But that is because the people making the movies need it to happen to make their jobs easier. It hardly ever happens in real life. Take it from me: If you ever need to get to or away from somewhere fast, and you jump into a strange car, and you see that the key is already in it, you're probably in a movie.

John dragged Cassie over to the car. It was unlocked, so he could open the door and peer in. "No key," he said. He slammed it shut and looked out toward the road. "Then we have to walk out of here until we come to a highway," he said. "And try to get somebody to stop and drive us into town." He noticed his sister hadn't said anything. She was standing there, thinking. "Right? Abby? Hello?"

She went over to him. "Dean D. Dean isn't going to meet Papa at the lab or at home. He's going to tell Papa that we're being held prisoner, and make Papa go somewhere with him where there won't be any people or police or anything."

John thought about that for *at most* half a second and said, "You're right. Dan said that Dean went to *pick up* Papa. We don't know where Dean will take him."

Just as John was about to sigh in frustration or flop his arms in an I-give-up gesture of despair, Abigail said, "Wait." And then she did the last thing he—or indeed you or I—would have expected her to do.

She went back into the house.

Isn't that unbelievable? It is. It's *unbelievable*. John just stood there, being shocked and finding it unbelievable. Then Abigail came running out of the house, carrying a piece of paper. She handed it to him. "I think this is where he's taking Papa."

John looked at the paper and said, basically, "Huh?"

This is what he saw:

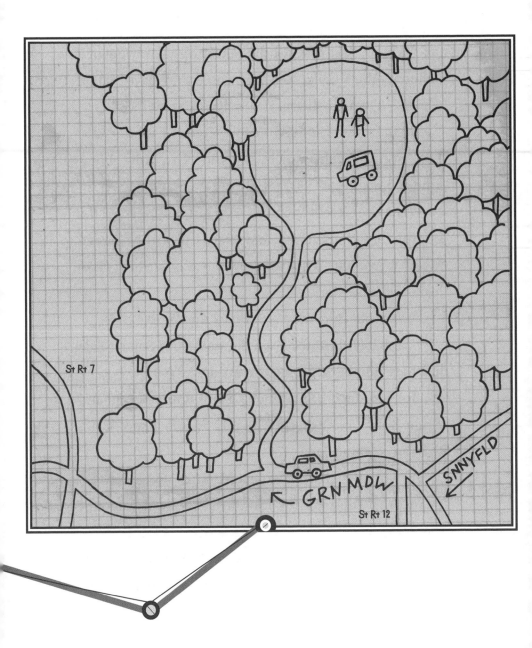

St Rt 7

← GRN MDW

SNNYFLD

St Rt 12

CHAPTER 12: THE TEMPLETON TWINS THINK OF SOMETHING
THAT EVEN THE NARRATOR HAS TO ADMIT IS CLEVER

"When I first saw it, I thought it was a drawing of a balloon," Abigail said. "But why would they leave that on a fridge? Then I looked at it closely. It's a map."

John frowned at the drawing. "How can it be a map? Look at these weird words. 'Snnyfld.' 'Grn Mdw.' What kind of map is that?"

"They're street names." Abigail pointed. "This is probably 'Sunnyfield' and this is probably 'Green Meadow Avenue.' Whoever drew this was in a hurry and just used abbreviations."

"Okay, but then what's 'St Rt 7'? And 'St Rt 12'?"

"Probably short for 'State Route Seven.' Some roads just have numbers instead of names."

John nodded. "So we have 'State Route Seven' and 'State Route Twelve.' Hey! Right! This is where Dean D. Dean is taking Papa—"

"—which means he expects Dan to go there, too. Dean drew the map for Dan. That's why it was still there."

The twins conferred. They could hike away from the Dean house in search of someone to help them, but there was no telling how long that might take.

And then John got an excellent idea, which was followed by Abigail getting a different excellent idea. Now, I cannot swear that John got his idea from a lesson he had learned from playing the drums. But it seems possible. So you tell me:

When you want to play something fast on the drums, the one thing you don't do is hold the sticks as tightly as you can and move your arms up and down as quickly as possible. You can get only a certain amount of speed that way, and not nearly as much speed as you would had you done it properly.

Instead, you hold the sticks in a certain way, and sort of *throw* their tips down onto the drumhead and *let them bounce*. Then you learn to control the bounces.

You don't force the sticks to move fast. You *allow* them to move fast. You let the sticks do what they "want" to do.

**BUT, NARRATOR!** you're probably about to say. "Drumsticks don't 'want' things! They're sticks." I know perfectly well that drumsticks are sticks. In addition, I am acquainted with the fact that sticks don't want things. That is why I put "want" in quotation marks. The quotation marks mean "in a sense, but not really."

We're getting off the point. And I blame you. Please, I urge you to stop interrupting. Instead, pay even more attention than usual as I describe for you what the twins figured out and how they solved their problem.

First, Abigail got into the car and peered at its dashboard until she saw what she had been looking for. "There," she said, pointing. "See?"

Then John reached into the car and found the control that opened the car's trunk. He opened the trunk. Abigail got inside the trunk and John closed the door— yes, all the way; yes, you heard me correctly: *He shut his own sister inside the trunk.*

Next, John looped Cassie's leash around the car bumper and went back into the house and put the map back on the refrigerator. He went up to the basement door and listened. He heard nothing, as though Dan D. Dean was taking a break from slamming into the door. So John quietly unlocked the door and left it open a little crack. Then he ran outside and threw himself on the ground and rolled around.

I know that you are upset at the news that John got his clothes even dirtier than he got them in the basement, but I have learned to make my peace with it, and I expect no less from you.

John sat on the ground until, a moment later, he heard the basement door bang open and saw Dan D. Dean run out into the front yard.

"I hurt my ankle," John said, rubbing his left ankle and acting like a twelve-year-old in great physical pain. (That was why he threw himself on the ground— to make it look as though he had stumbled and hurt his ankle.)

"Where's the girl?" Dan D. Dean said.

"She ran out to the highway to get help."

Dan D. Dean stood there for a second, breathing hard and being infuriated. He ran inside and came out a moment later with the map. Then he grabbed John by the arm and dragged him over to the car. "Get in," he said, and flung John into the backseat. Dan disgustedly unhooked Cassie from the bumper, and the *still* ridiculous dog leaped in after John, thrilled and ecstatic and ready for fun.

Dan D. Dean got in and, *with the key that he had had in his possession the whole time, as people do in real life,* started the car, turned it around in a cloud of dust and with a squeal of tires, and roared up the dirt road.

They came to the main highway, and Dan D. Dean looked back and forth. "I don't see her," he said.

"Great!" John said. "That means someone picked her up!"

Dan D. Dean gritted his teeth and floored the accelerator, and the car zoomed down the highway. Cassie, as she always did, wasted no time in wriggling into the front seat and climbing on the driver's lap. "Get this animal off me!" Dan D. Dean yelled. John took Cassie in his arms and held her on his lap. As they drove, he thought about how clever his sister was.

For once I wouldn't blame you if you don't understand what I'm referring to. So let me explain.

It had been John's idea to let Dan D. Dean loose and, as when he let a drumstick bounce the way it "wanted" to, to allow him to drive where he wanted to—which, they were sure, was where his brother, Dean D. Dean, had taken the Professor. John had then suggested that he and his sister hide in the trunk of the car.

But Abigail, with the swiftness of mind that comes from working on cryptic crossword puzzles, had realized that there was a fatal flaw in that plan.

Had both the Templeton twins jumped in the trunk and shut the trunk door, they would have been unable to get out of the trunk when they got to their destination. (Or, they would have had to make noise and yell, "Let us out!" enabling the Dean brothers—the Dean *twins*—to take them prisoner, which would accomplish nothing.) But had they left the trunk door open a crack, Dan D. Dean would have seen the little light on the dashboard that tells you when the trunk (or a door) isn't fully closed. That's what Abigail was looking for on the dashboard— that little "a door is open" light. If Dan D. Dean had seen it, he would have stopped the car, looked in the trunk, and discovered the twins.

So it had been Abigail's idea that one of them ride in the fully closed trunk, and the other with Dan D. Dean. They knew that he would join his brother as quickly as possible once he thought that one of the twins had gotten away.

He would want to know why John hadn't escaped with Abigail, so they made up the story that John had hurt his ankle.

Yes, it was very clever. Forgive me, but I'm sure *you* wouldn't be capable of thinking up something as clever as that. And, frankly, I'm not sure I would be, either.

They drove and drove. Actually, they didn't drive and drive. They just drove, for about fifteen minutes. John noted with satisfaction that they drove down Sunnyfield Road, turned right onto Green Meadow Avenue, and passed State Route Twelve. Alas, they never saw State Route Seven because, before they came to it, they turned right, onto a dirt and grass road that led into an area of thick forest.

They bounded and bounced across this rutted, rocky road for about five minutes. John wondered if Abigail, in the trunk, was being terribly banged around by the car's wild bouncing and decided that she probably was. He felt bad for her, but what could he do?

Then the car reached a clearing in the forest, and John saw everything that he had hoped he would and wouldn't see.

The black SUV was there. Professor Templeton was there, wearing his usual baggy white trousers and billowing white shirt and looking frightened but trying to bear up under the circumstances. And Dean D. Dean was there, standing next to the Professor, pointing a gun at him.

Dan D. Dean stopped his car and snarled, "Get out." John put Cassie on the ground and then got out, making sure to remember to limp and hobble and act as though he suffered from a hurt ankle. He made his way around toward the driver's side, leaned against it, and sulked, as though he didn't know what to do and was full of despair. Dan D. Dean got out, said, "Let's go," and marched off to join his brother.

That's when John had a moment to reach in and, using the control near the driver's door, open the trunk. Then he fake-limped off toward the others. Cassie, seeing Professor Templeton there, wagged her absurd tail and looked energized and delighted. Behind him, as he went, John could sense his sister sneaking out of the trunk and quietly lowering its lid.

They had now reached the second phase of their Plan, which I am calling Phase II.

## QUESTIONS FOR REVIEW

1. The twins' scheme to hide Abigail in the trunk was clever, but weren't you impressed by how clearly the Narrator explained it?

2. When John got his clothes extremely dirty while escaping from the basement and rolling around on the ground to seem injured, wasn't it horrible?

3. Essay Question: Write an essay on how clever you think you are. It should be at least 500,000 words and in French. Well, go ahead.

THE TEMPLETON TWINS HAVE AN IDEA

# CHAPTER 13

# VARIOUS UNEXPECTED THINGS OCCUR

D ean D. Dean stood across from Professor Temple-ton, pointing the gun at him. John pretended to hobble over to where they stood.

"John!" the Professor cried, hurrying toward his son. "Are you all right? You're hurt!"

"I'm fine, Papa," John said.

"Where is Abigail?"

"She got away," John said. He didn't enjoy lying to his father, but he decided that that wasn't exactly what he was doing. He was lying to the Dean twins. His father was an innocent bystander, an innocent listener, a bystand-ing listener—oh, just never mind.

"Excuse me?" Dean D. Dean said to his brother. "She got *away?*"

"It's not my fault!" Dan D. Dean said.

"Of course it is," John said. "Who else's fault could it be?"

With his eyes rolled toward the sky and in a long-suffering, this-happens-all-the-time tone, Dean D. Dean asked his brother, "Where is she now?"

"How should I know?" Dan D. Dean cried. "I came outside and she was gone!" He pointed to John. "*He* was still there because he hurt his foot."

"She's getting the police," John said.

Dan D. Dean looked frightened and panicky. "Dean! She's getting the police!?"

"Oh, don't be a big baby." His brother gestured in an open, innocent fashion to the woods all around them, as though to say, "We are doing nothing wrong."

"We are doing nothing wrong! What are we doing? We're standing here on a nice afternoon in the woods, chatting nicely and signing papers. What are we doing that's not perfectly legal?"

"Kidnapping isn't legal," John said.

"He's right!" Dan D. Dean cried. "Kidnapping is against the law!"

"Who said anything about kidnapping?" Dean D. Dean said.

"You kidnapped us!" John said.

Dean D. Dean made a don't-be-absurd face and shook his head. **"OH, PLEASE,"** he said. "We did nothing of the kind. We came to your house, and we took you and your sister for a visit to our house! That kind of thing happens all the time. What's the big deal?"

"That's not all you did," John said.

"I—oh, all right, have it your way," Dean D. Dean said in a tone of voice that suggested he was trying very, very hard to be fair. "We locked you in the basement. So what? You got out, didn't you? So what's so kidnappy about that?"

"You killed Nanny Nan," John said. "Murder is against the law, too."

"He's right!" Dan D. Dean cried. "Murder *is* against the law!"

"Honestly!" Dean D. Dean said. "We didn't murder anyone. We tried to, yes. But we missed!"

"You gave her a heart attack," John said.

"No, she gave herself a heart attack. We just happened to be standing there. And so were you! And so was your sister. For that matter—" he said, pointing to Cassie, who had stretched out on the ground with her head up, looking at the surrounding woods with great interest, "—so was this dog. Are you going to put your dog in jail for murder? I don't think so!" Dean D. Dean waved the gun at the Professor and at the papers. "Sign them."

"Dean," Dan D. Dean said. "What if the girl does go to the police?"

"Relax," his brother said. "It'll take her all day. She'll have to hitchhike. And she doesn't know where we are anyway."

The Professor's face turned white with fear. He looked at Dean D. Dean. "Hitchhike? Abigail? Oh, dear." John wanted to tell him not to be concerned, that Abigail was at that very moment hiding near the metallic blue car a hundred feet away. But of course he couldn't. The Professor said in a frighteningly serious voice, "If either of these children is hurt, you will regret it for the rest of your life."

"They're fine!" Dean D. Dean said. He pointed to John. "Look! And the girl got away!"

The Professor said to John, "You're sure you're all right?"

John nodded. The Professor, still worried, clamped his lips shut, put his glasses back on, and began reading the documents.

John looked around. That's when he saw, lying nearby on the ground, a strange-looking object. He knew immediately what it was.

Yes, it was the Personal One-Man Helicopter (POMH) prototype. The device was complete: the motor, the controls, the rotors, and, of course, the knapsack.

"Just sign it," Dean D. Dean said again. "I told you, it's the usual thing. You share all ownership and profits with me. By 'share,' in this case, I mean 'give all to me.'"

"I don't sign anything before I read it," the Professor said.

"What if he doesn't sign?" John said.

Dean D. Dean went over to John and held up the gun for him to see. He said, in a quiet, menacing voice, "Then someone might get hurt. It might be him, or it might be you."

The Professor looked up at Dean D. Dean. "There's a problem," he said. "I can't sign this."

"Oh, yes, you can!" Dean D. Dean said. "And you'd better, Mister Professor Big Shot Templeton. I'm starting to lose patience."

"No, I mean I can't sign it," the Professor said.

"I'm warning you!"

"I mean I don't have a pen."

Dean D. Dean started snapping his fingers at John and at Dan D. Dean, saying, "Pen. Pen. Pen. Somebody give him a pen."

"I don't have a pen, Dean," Dan D. Dean said.

"How can you not have a pen!?"

"I just don't."

"You," Dean D. Dean said to John. "You have a pen. You're a student! Students have pens!"

"I don't have one," John said.

"And you flunked *me?!*" Dean D. Dean yelled at the Professor. "Why don't you try flunking your own son? He doesn't even have a pen!"

"Perhaps you have one," the Professor said.

"Oh, for goodness' sake!" Dean D. Dean said and slapped himself on the chest. "Oh. As a matter of fact, I do." He reached into his jacket pocket and pulled out a ballpoint pen. "How about that!" he laughed, handing the pen to the Professor.

That's when they heard a car door slam shut.

Everyone jumped. Dean D. Dean spun around and looked toward the black SUV and, beyond it, the metallic blue car. He turned to his brother and said, "Check it out."

"Me? Why me?"

"Because I'm witnessing the signature. Just do it."

Dan D. Dean looked nervous but started walking toward the cars. John took that opportunity to kneel down and to pretend to tie his shoe.

Dan D. Dean approached the black SUV warily, but the more he looked it over, the more he relaxed. There was nothing amiss with it. Satisfied that it had not been the source of the sound, he turned his attention toward the metallic blue car.

He approached the vehicle very slowly. Nothing seemed to be wrong. It was empty. All the doors were closed—well, not quite. The lid of the trunk was half open. That made no sense. It looked suspicious. It looked *wrong*.

Dan D. Dean slowly walked along the passenger side of the car with his eyes fixed on the half-open trunk. Suddenly he leaped forward and flung the trunk completely open. Inside was an odd and unexpected thing. It was a pair of pink shoes. Dan D. Dean bent over and reached out to pick them up.

E.

01

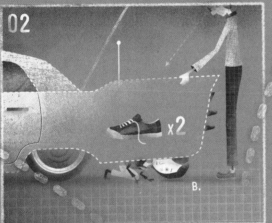

02

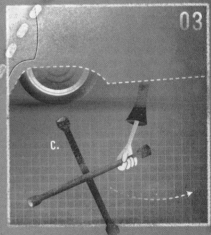

03

04

He heard a vague, odd rustling as a shape emerged from underneath the car. Then the shape took a whack at his leg with something hard, and the next thing he knew he was rolling on the ground in extreme pain.

He heard a girl yell, "This way, detective!"

That was when John, having finished pretending to tie his shoe, grabbed a rock he had spotted on the ground, jumped up, and slammed it down onto the gun hand of Dean D. Dean. The handsome man dropped the gun with a cry—and John immediately fell on it as though it were a football or a rugby ball or some other kind of ball people fall on.

Abigail ran up to them. She was holding her shoes, which she had retrieved when Dan D. Dean dropped them after she had whacked him in the leg with a tire iron from the trunk. Do you know what a tire iron is? In fact, it's—look, never mind. Things are much too exciting for me to explain it now. Ask someone to tell you after you have finished reading this book.

Abigail put her shoes on. "It worked!" she said.

**"OH, PLEASE,"** Dean D. Dean said in a sort of tired, bored manner. He walked over to the Professor and suddenly grabbed him, whipped the Professor's arm behind his back, and pressed his other arm across the Professor's throat. "It didn't 'work.' What are you going to do—shoot your father? I don't think so! Give me that gun."

"Forget it!" John said.

Abigail leaned toward her brother and said, "I have an idea. Give it to me."

John handed the gun to his sister. She examined it carefully and found the little tab that flips open and allows you to put new bullets into the round, turning part of the gun which, when you shoot the gun, automatically revolves a bit and gets the next bullet into position to be fired. (That is why this kind of gun is called a "revolver." See? Aren't some things obvious once you know them?)

Abigail shook out the bullets one by one as Dean D. Dean said, "Hey! That's private property!" When she had removed five full bullets and one empty shell (left over from when Dean D. Dean had shot at Nanny Nan), she turned, ran into the woods a few feet, and threw them as far as she could.

Dean D. Dean watched this with what we may agree was understandable dismay. He snarled, "That is outrageous! You go find those bullets and bring them back at once, young lady!"

Which, of course, Abigail did not do. Instead, she came back to Dean D. Dean and held out the gun, handle first. She indicated her father and said, "Now let him go."

Dean D. Dean made a noise of anger and frustration. Then he shoved the Professor away from him, seized the gun, turned his back to everyone, and reached into his pocket. He seemed to pull out something, and then did something with the gun. Something clicked. He turned back to the Templetons and aimed the gun at them.

"I had one extra bullet," he said.

"Oh, baloney!" Abigail said. "You did not!"

"Want to try me, little girl?"

Suddenly everyone heard *another* car door slam. They all spun around just in time to see the black SUV roar to life. It plowed twin (!) furrows in the wet, mossy earth as it made a fast U-turn and started driving away.

"Hey!" Dean D. Dean yelled. He ran toward it shouting, "I don't—! Wait!" But the driver (who, we are safe in assuming, was his twin brother, Dan D. Dean) apparently didn't care. The black SUV drove off down the rutted road until it could no longer be seen or heard.

Dean D. Dean looked grim as he stomped back to rejoin the Templetons. He thought for a second, and then pointed the gun at the Professor and thumbed toward the Personal One-Man Helicopter prototype. "Help me get into that," he snarled.

"Don't do it, Papa!" Abigail cried. "He's lying about the extra bullet!"

"I don't care, dear," Professor Templeton said. "All that matters is that you two are safe. Come on, Mr. Dean. And for once in your life pay close attention when I explain something."

Professor Templeton gave the document to Abigail to hold as he reviewed how the Personal One-Man Helicopter worked. John helped him lift up and steady its knapsack as Dean D. Dean (still pointing the gun at Abigail) got into it.

You may be thinking, "Quick! While Dean D. Dean is distracted with the helicopter and off-balance because it's so heavy and everything, someone should *do* something!"

But if the twins thought about trying to do something, they decided it wasn't worth the risk. Yes, it occurred to both the twins and their father that Dean D. Dean might have pulled nothing at all from his pants pocket and might be bluffing about the extra bullet. But if he wasn't bluffing, whatever they could gain by *doing* something wasn't worth his shooting them—even by accident, during a moment of panic or anger.

Finally the motor of the Personal One-Man Helicopter was on Dean D. Dean's back. Its controls, with their wires leading out of the knapsack, were in his hands. (They were, you will be amused to learn, not unlike the controls of a PlayBox or an X-Station, or whatever those video games are that you people find so enthralling.) The rotor blades that would enable him to rise and fly forward were extended. "It's all gassed up and everything?" Dean D. Dean asked.

"As I explained, it's battery operated," the Professor said. "And its battery is charged, yes."

"Good. Now sign."

"I am still reading," the Professor said.

"Okay, fine, yes, please, keep reading," Dean D. Dean said. "Meanwhile I am going to practice using this thing." He turned a key on the control panel and pushed a button.

The motor in the knapsack revved up into an annoying drone like the kind made by radio-controlled model airplanes. Dean D. Dean said **HAH!**, and moved a control.

Instantly the rotor above his head started turning around faster and faster until suddenly he lifted off the ground. "YAHH! WAHH!" he cried. "Okay . . . okay . . ." He worked the controls until he stopped rising and hovered about twenty feet off the ground in his lovely tan slacks and beige jacket. The turning rotor made a downward wind that mussed up his hair, but he didn't mind.

Dean D. Dean worked another control, and the smaller rotor, like a little fan sticking out the back of the knapsack, began to turn, moving him forward. He practiced steering and rising and descending. His body wobbled and sometimes he turned almost upside down, but soon he seemed to understand how to control the device.

(While Dean D. Dean is practicing with the POMH, I invite you to sneak a glance at Abigail. She had been absently staring at Cassie, not really looking at her but sort of taking a break from all the scary and demanding things that had gone on all day. And then, all at once, she came out of her reverie and focused sharply on the Ridiculous Dog, who was lying there breathing normally, as though this were just another pleasant family outing. As is so often the case, Abigail had just had an idea.)

Meanwhile, Dean D. Dean came in for a landing. He staggered a bit but managed to stay on his feet. **"THIS IS EASY!"** he said, laughing. Then he pulled the gun from his jacket pocket and pointed it at the Professor. "Enough reading, old man," he said. "Sign. NOW."

The Professor sighed and, with the pen Dean D. Dean had given him, signed the last page of the document. He handed the pen and the pages to Dean D. Dean and said, "There. Now go away and don't bother us ever again."

"Finally. Excellent. And now, if you'll excuse me—and even if you won't!— **I AM OUTTA HERE.**

Abigail said, "Wait." She got a look of smarty-pants cleverness on her face and said to Dean D. Dean, "You can fly away all you want. It won't do any good. John has gone for the police."

John Templeton, who in fact was two feet away, holding Cassie's leash, started to say something but stopped himself. Something, he knew, was Up.

"What are you talking about?" Dean D. Dean said.

"John. My brother. He got away while you were up in the air, and he's gone for the police."

"Are you crazy?" Dean D. Dean said. "He's standing right there."

"Oh, really? Where?"

Dean D. Dean extended an elegantly jacketed arm toward John and pointed his finger. "Right *there.*"

This proved to be a bad idea.

As soon as Dean D. Dean pointed at John, Cassie leaped to her feet and bared her sharp white fox terrier teeth and strained against the leash to get at the person pointing at a Templeton twin. Dean D. Dean froze in fear and cried, "Don't let her off the leash!"

"Okay!" John answered. "I won't!" Because he didn't have to, you see. A leash works only if there's someone at the other end of it. All John had to do was let go of the leash. Which he did.

Cassie ran at Dean D. Dean and snapped at his leg. He pointed the gun at her.

And then he pulled the trigger.

## QUESTIONS FOR REVIEW

1. Do you have a pen?

2. What do you mean, "no"?

3. Fill in the blank: The Narrator is doing an excellent job, and I am very grateful to him. (Hint: This is a trick question. In fact, it's so tricky, it's not a question at all. This *statement* needs no filling in, and there is no blank to fill in. But it expresses a lovely sentiment with which I'm sure you'll agree.)

# CHAPTER 14

# THE TEMPLETON TWINS HAVE THE BEST IDEA OF THEM ALL

T here was . . . not exactly a BANG. In fact, it was more like a click. Nothing happened.

"I knew it!" Abigail said.

Cassie had now managed to sink her teeth into a leg of Dean D. Dean's lovely trousers. The One-Man Helicoptering man frantically threw the gun aside, grabbed the controls, turned the key, and pressed the button. The overhead rotor started turning. Slowly, Dean D. Dean rose into the air, with the little white dog still attached to his leg and snarling. Dean D. Dean shook his leg to get the dog to let go. But one of the famously distinctive things about terriers is: They don't let go.

"Off! Off! Off! Off!" Dean D. Dean cried at the ridiculous, tenacious dog. Then he tried to bend down and remove Cassie from his leg. That was when he dropped the document, which fluttered down to the ground like . . . well, like a sheaf of papers falling to the ground.

John ran to retrieve the papers. Abigail ran under Dean D. Dean and the dog and cried, "Cassie! Here! Cookie! Cookie!"

I see, above, that I said that terriers don't let go. The precise fact of the matter is, they *usually* don't let go. But a terrier, like most dogs, will do practically anything for a dog biscuit or a "cookie." Cassie, believing (ridiculously) that Abigail was offering her a treat, opened her mouth and fell into Abigail's arms.

"Finally!" Dean D. Dean shouted. "And now, goodbye and good riddance!"

"Wait!" Now it was John's turn to have an idea. Before Dean D. Dean could speak again or fly off, John called, "What about the battery charger?" Then he said, "Oops!" and clamped his hand to his mouth.

Everybody looked at everybody else. "What is he talking about?" Dean D. Dean asked.

"Nothing," John said. He waved at Dean D. Dean and cried, "Bye! Have a nice flight!"

Dean D. Dean descended a bit and fixed John with a stern, I'm-an-adult-and-you're-a-child look. "What charger?"

John shook his head and waved his hands in a manner that suggested he was blabbing on about silly trifles. "Nothing. Forget it. It's at the lab." He looked at this father very intently and said, "Right? Isn't that where the charger is? *At the lab?*"

Professor Templeton opened his mouth to speak, but then gave his son a thoughtful, frowning look and shut it. Abigail, who realized that something was Up, put Cassie on the ground and watched her brother with wide eyes.

"*What battery charger?!*" Dean D. Dean demanded.

"The problem is the battery," John said. "Isn't that what you've been working on, Papa?"

"Um, I, ah, that is, eh, ah—" the Professor said.

"The power source?" John said urgently. "That you've been working on?"

"Well, yes, but, you see, batteries of this scale are so heavy, we . . . " And then the Professor grew silent. He looked at John and seemed to figure something out. Suddenly he smiled and continued, "In fact, you see—it's quite interesting, really, Mr. Dean—converting the chemical electrical energy of a battery into the *kinetic* energy of turning blades is a most cumbersome and challenging—"

**SHUT UP!** Dean D. Dean yelled. "Where is this thing, and why do I need it?"

"Oh, good going, John," Abigail said in what I can assure you was a most sarcastic fashion. "Now you have to tell him."

"All right," John said, sounding embarrassed and ashamed at having revealed something he should have kept to himself. "If you want to go any distance at all," he said to Dean D. Dean, "you'll have to go Papa's lab and get the charger to recharge the battery."

"And now I suppose you're going to tell him it's on the main lab table," Abigail said.

"Well . . . " John suddenly brightened and became visibly—or *apparently*—happy. "It doesn't matter!" he told his sister. "He doesn't know where the lab is!"

"Of course I know where the lab is!" Dean D. Dean barked.

I am going to pause now and point out something that you may or may not have noticed.

When John asked, "What about the battery charger?" you may, if you are quite clever (which is to say, nearly as clever as I am), have suddenly thought, "Huh? Why is John helping Dean D. Dean get away?" Or had he made a mistake? After all, John tried—or seemed to try—to take it back and forget the whole thing. And you will also have noticed, from the brilliant way I have described this scene, that Professor Templeton himself was wondering this, too. That is why his first answer to John's question was "Um, ha, hoo, ah, hee, um . . . " or words to that effect. He was, as we say, stalling.

Then you will have noticed that Abigail abruptly said things that not only supported what John had said, but added even more. She told John that he "had to" tell Dean D. Dean what the charger was for. But why? Why did John "have to" reveal anything?

Plus, you will have noticed that Abigail *herself* told Dean D. Dean something—that the charger was "on the main lab table." Why? Why would Abigail actually assist her brother in telling their enemy things he would need to know in order to escape?

The answer, as you will see, is that Abigail *realized* *what her brother had in mind and she thought that his idea just might work.*

I don't expect you to know what that idea was. You would have to be even more intelligent than I am to be able to guess what John's scheme was. And I think the odds of that being the case are rather small, don't you?

"Thanks for the tip, kid!" Dean D. Dean shouted. "I'm getting that charger and then I am GONE!" And he flew off over the trees.

"Quick!" John said. "Let's go!"

"Wait," Abigail said. **WE NEED A PLAN.**

"We don't have time to stand around thinking of a *plan!* We have to do something!"

"John, we won't know what to *do* until we think of it first!"

"Children," the Professor said. "You're both correct. But even if we had a plan, how could we go anywhere?" He pointed to the metallic blue car. "Dan D. Dean has driven off with this car's keys."

"Oh," John said. "Right."

"Unless . . . " The Professor looked thoughtful and started walking toward the car.

The Templeton twins traded a fast look. Then, because it didn't seem like a good idea to leave an actual gun lying around in the woods, John retrieved the actual gun. They ran after their father. "Unless what?" Abigail said.

"This is an old car," the Professor said. "I might be able to hot-wire it."

Now, Professor Templeton knew everything there was to know about engines and motors. If anyone could hot-wire the car, it—

I'm sorry, what? Is it possible you don't know what "hot-wiring" a car means? How very disappointing. And yet I know exactly what it means. Isn't that fascinating?

To "hot-wire" a car means to break into its controls and manipulate its wiring so that the car can be started without a key. You connect the starter to the ignition or the battery to the alternator or the whatsis to the thingie. Look, I don't know *exactly* how it works. All I know is, you are able to start and drive the car without the key, all right?

"Good!" John yelled. "Do it! Fast!"

"It will be a pleasure," the Professor said. "Abby, get me that tire iron."

Professor Templeton got behind the wheel of the metallic blue car, then whacked the steering column, which is the part of the car that holds up the steering wheel. A panel immediately fell off the column, revealing all the wires and switches and things that made the car start.

The Professor took from his pocket the Swiss Army knife that he always carried—one of those red pocket-knives that contain five or ten or even twenty (or more, if you can believe it) different blades and tools. I am sure you know what a Swiss Army knife is. But can you tell me, please, why the Swiss (who live in Switzerland, which is a tiny country with no enemies whatsoever) need to have an army? And why the army has to carry around big, complicated knives full of screwdrivers and wine openers and nail files and scissors and Allen wrenches and toothpicks? No, you cannot. LET'S MOVE ON.

The Professor pulled out some wires, cut into them, and tied them to each other, and in less than fifteen seconds the metallic blue car started with a loud, deep roar.

The twins cheered and slapped their father on the back. Then John and Abigail got into the rear seat, Cassie got in next to the Professor in the front, all the humans buckled their seat belts, Cassie jumped into the Professor's lap, and they drove briskly out of the woods.

They reached the main highway and stopped. The Professor looked in one direction and then the other. "I'm not quite sure where we are, children," he said.

"Look!" Abigail said.

She pointed ahead of them, and up. There, flying at about the level of the treetops, was Dean D. Dean in the Personal One-Man Helicopter.

"That way!" John cried. ◄ **FOLLOW *HIM!***

Of course, it was impossible to literally follow Dean D. Dean, since *he* was not following the highway. That's the point of a flying machine, you see: You don't have to stay on roads. But that didn't matter. As long as he was heading in the direction of the campus of Tick-Tock Tech, they knew which roads to follow.

The Professor hit the gas and they zoomed off. As they drove, he asked, "But why are we rushing? Shouldn't we stop and call the police?"

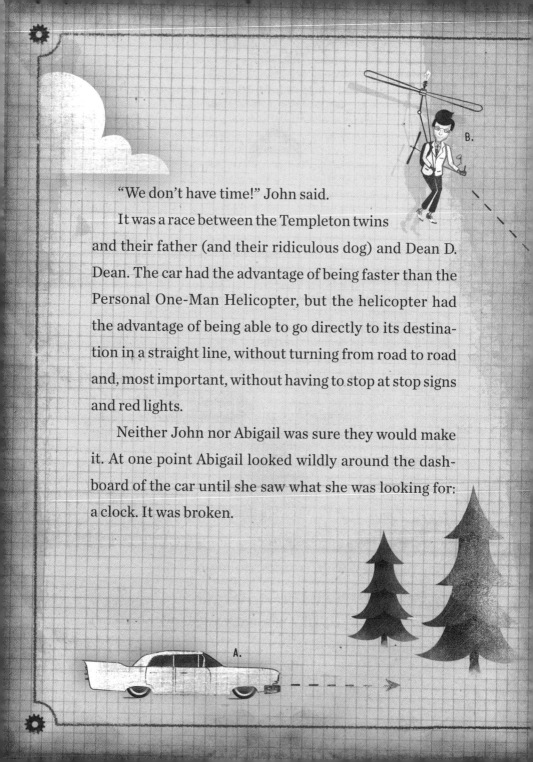

"We don't have time!" John said.

It was a race between the Templeton twins and their father (and their ridiculous dog) and Dean D. Dean. The car had the advantage of being faster than the Personal One-Man Helicopter, but the helicopter had the advantage of being able to go directly to its destination in a straight line, without turning from road to road and, most important, without having to stop at stop signs and red lights.

Neither John nor Abigail was sure they would make it. At one point Abigail looked wildly around the dashboard of the car until she saw what she was looking for: a clock. It was broken.

B.

A.

"Oh, Papa, what time is it?" she asked.

The Professor looked at his watch. "It's twelve minutes before four, dear. Why?"

Abigail looked at John. "We don't have much time," John said. "Papa, can you drive any faster?"

The Professor drove faster, and soon they arrived. They turned into the entrance of the campus, which was, as usual, deserted.

They drove to Jerry Hall and parked in front just as Dean D. Dean floated into view. When he saw the metallic blue car waiting for him, he gave such a start that he almost dropped the controls and plunged to the ground. But he recovered and stopped, hovering about sixty feet in the air over the center of the main quad.

"Go after him, Papa," John said. "Drive onto the grass."

The Professor hesitated. "Is . . . is that truly necessary?" he asked.

"Yes! Please!" Abigail said. "And then we have to get out and tell him we want to give him the papers."

"Abby, for goodness' sake, why would we do that?"

"Oh, hurry, Papa, drive out to where he is. Before he gives up and just flies away!"

Professor Templeton made a look of doubt and confusion, then slowly drove the metallic blue car up and over the curb and onto the grass and down a small slope and out onto the big, broad, grassy field, where Dean D. Dean remained hovering.

I will now pause and permit you to guess what is going to happen next. I seriously doubt that you will be able to do so. Moreover, if afterward you tell me that you *were* able to guess correctly what did in fact happen next, I simply will not believe you. Why should I? Nonetheless, now is your chance. Go on.

## QUESTIONS FOR REVIEW

1. What do you think will happen next?

2. Did you think of that yourself, or did you have help?

3. Why should I believe you?

CHAPTER 15

# JUST ABOUT EVERYTHING COMES TOGETHER AT THE SAME TIME

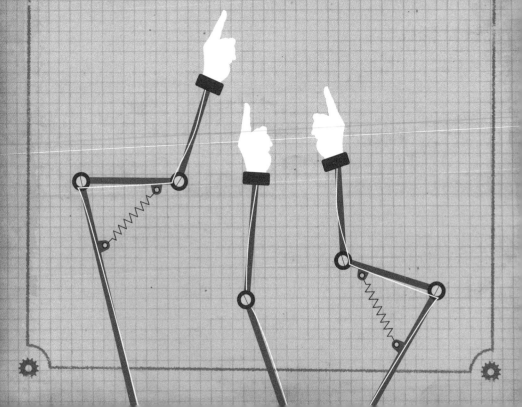

A bigail jumped out of the car and waved the papers at Dean D. Dean as he hovered in the air. Then John took Cassie off his father's lap and got out of the car, too. Cassie stood beside John, on the leash, looking up at the hovering, handsome, horrible man and barking.

"We changed our mind!" Abigail shouted up to him. "We're going to give you these!"

"Oh, really?" he said. "And why is that?"

She quickly turned around and looked behind her, past the car, past the two tracks of mashed grass the car had made while driving across the field, and up at the clock tower on Jerry Hall. Then she turned back to Dean D. Dean and said, "Because, um, because—"

"Because Papa remembered that you said, 'Put it in a backpack'!" John called.

"KNAPSACK!" Dean D. Dean shouted. "Not back-pack. I *said,* 'Put it in a knapsack!'"

"Knapsack, fine," John yelled. "But if we give you this, do you promise you won't bother us anymore?"

"Well, that is more like it," Dean D. Dean called. "Yes! I promise! But I'm not coming down until you get that dog out of here!"

John yelled back, "Okay!" but then, rather than moving Cassie somewhere else, he looked all around the field they were on, went over to Abigail, and told her something. She nodded. The two of them (and, of course, the ridiculous dog) walked with very deliberate care about twelve feet to their left and then about eight feet straight ahead.

"Hey!" Dean D. Dean cried. "Where are you going?" He had to work the Personal One-Man Helicopter's controls to reposition himself and continue his conversation with the twins. He drifted over until he was once again above and slightly ahead of them.

John muttered to Abigail, "How much longer?"

She now stood right next to her brother, back to back. He faced Dean D. Dean. She faced Jerry Hall. **"TEN SECONDS,"** she said quietly.

"GET RID OF THE DOG—"

**"NINE SECONDS."**

"—AND I'LL COME DOWN," Dean D. Dean shouted.

**"EIGHT."**

"I want those papers AND I want the battery charger!"

## "SEVEN."

"What battery charger?" John called up to him.

## "SIX."

"WHAT DO YOU MEAN, WHAT BATTERY CH—"

## "FIVE."

John called back, "What?"

## "FOUR."

"I *said*," Dean D. Dean shouted, "What do you—"

## "THREE."

"—mean, what battery charger?"

## "TWO."

"What?"

## "ONE."

"I SAID—"

## "NOW!"

There was a loud clack-clang-crack as all the minute hands on all the clocks on all the buildings all across the Tickeridge-Baltock Institute of Technology reached twelve and all the hour hands snapped to four. The chimes and bells and bongs and gongs and cuckoos all sounded the fact that it was four o'clock.

"Hey!" Dean D. Dean yelled. "Wait a minute—"

Whatever he proceeded to say next was drowned out by the sound of doors flying open all across campus and the din of hundreds of students flooding out of their buildings, talking and laughing and shouting and singing and blah blah blah. As before, many of them swarmed toward other buildings and entered, one by one, in ticktock regularity, for their next classes.

But also, as before, many of them were finished with classes for the day. They dispersed throughout the campus to lounge around and loaf about. And . . .

. . . to throw Frisbees.

Just as on the day before, the Frisbee throwers deployed around the open field. And, just as on the day before, as though in response to an invisible, silent, secret signal, all the Frisbee throwers threw their Frisbees at the same time, and all the Frisbees flew up toward the same place in the air.

And they all smacked into the hovering Dean D. Dean.

"Stop! Stop! Stop! Ouch! Stop!" he cried.

He took both hands off the controls to swat and swing at the Frisbees as they all zipped and wobbled into him like a flock of colorful plastic birds. Some Frisbees hit the overhead rotor and caused it to shake and flap. One hit the rear rotor and jammed in it, causing it to stop turning altogether. Without the controls and rotors, only one thing could happen. And it did.

Dean D. Dean, shouting **AAAAHHHH!**, plunged to Earth.

He landed on his feet and tried to roll forward, as though doing a somersault, but the Personal One-Man Helicopter threw off his balance and completely tangled him up. So all he did was crash in a heap. The droning of the motors stopped. The happy, jokey shouting of the Frisbee throwers stopped. In fact, the whole field became silent.

Then the silence was shattered by the Templeton twins shouting, "Yaaay!" and the Professor murmuring, "My goodness."

Dean D. Dean staggered to his feet, tore off the knapsack, and flung the Personal One-Man Helicopter to the ground. He tried to run at the Templetons, but after a single step one leg buckled under him. Possibly it was broken. In any case, he lost his footing and collapsed onto the ground.

"Now we can call the police," John said.

"Wait a minute," Abigail said. "What's that noise?"

It was a combination of a roaring motor and a blaring car horn. They looked around until they saw its source: Charging into the driveway of the campus, barreling up the road toward Jerry Hall, and then bouncing and blaring at them over the same part of the field that they had driven across came the black SUV.

**UH-OH**, John said.

The black SUV roared past the twins and their father out into the center of the field, where it stopped next to the collapsed Dean D. Dean. The driver—who, as you very well might have guessed, was Dan D. Dean—got out, ran around to the passenger's side, opened the door, and helped his brother get in.

Then Dan D. Dean shut the door, ran back to the driver's side, got in, shut his door, threw the car into gear, and drove off with a loud rev of the engine, leaving behind a wake of torn-up grass. In seconds the black SUV was gone.

## QUESTIONS FOR REVIEW

1. Did you guess what was going to happen?

2. No, you didn't.

3. Please. Don't embarrass yourself. **LET'S MOVE ON.**

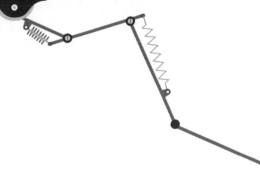

# CHAPTER 16

# A SURPRISE, AN ANSWER, AN END

T here was not much left to do but collect the wreckage of the One-Man Personal Helicopter and take it to the Professor's lab. Then the Professor and the Templeton twins (and C., the R. D.) got into the Professor's car (which had been left at Tick-Tock Tech when Dean D. Dean had shown up to take the Professor to their conference in the woods) and drove home.

On the way they were somewhat somber. Yes, they were safe, and it was unlikely they would ever again be bothered by Dean D. Dean or his brother. But the prospect of going home reminded them of the terrible fate of Nanny Nan. The excitement and relief and satisfaction of having outwitted the Dean twins had been soon replaced by a brooding silence.

When they turned the corner onto their street, Abigail said, "Look. That's funny. . . " There was a police car in front of the house. And it was funny—meaning "strange," not "amusing"—because no one, not even Nanny Nan when she made her phone call before Dean D. Dean tried to shoot her, had called the police.

"Someone must have heard the gunshot and called them," John said as they climbed the porch steps.

"Yes," their father agreed, reaching for his keys. "But too late to save poor Nanny Nan."

At that the front door flew open and a tall, thin figure in gray pants and a gray shirt and a black baseball cap said: "So. THERE you are. Well, good. The children look safe and sound, and that's what's important. But I must say, I don't care for the way I've been treated today. Left unconscious for HOURS! Did it not occur to any of you to phone the police? Must I do everything myself?"

Professor Templeton's eyes lit up with relief. "Miss Noonan! You . . . I mean to say, you're alive!"

"No thanks to any of you, I may say," said Nanny Nan (for it was indeed she) as she turned and called into the house, "Yes, Officer Timmons, it's the Professor and the twins.

A tired-looking policeman in uniform appeared. He smiled, shrugged, and said, "Folks, we—" and that was all he managed to get out.

"It is absolutely beyond me that no one bothered to check on my condition. I lay on that kitchen floor for four hours!"

"We were kidnapped!" Abigail said.

"Plus, we thought you were dead," John said. "From a heart attack."

"I may as well have *been* dead, for all anyone cared," Nanny Nan said. "It so happens I was not dead. I fainted."

The twins were momentarily stymied. Finally Abigail said, "Really? You fainted? Do people really faint?"

"Of course I fainted! Kidnappers running around, dogs barking, guns going off—what else is there to do *but* faint?"

The Professor tried to restore quiet. "Yes, well," he said. "The important thing now is that you are all right." He moved as though to walk into the house.

But Nanny Nan did not budge. "No, the important thing is, I cannot remain in the employ of people with such an alarming and, if you must know, CRIMINAL class of acquaintances."

"Acquaintances?" Abigail said. "Those aren't our acquaintances. They're two horrible brothers we had never even met before!"

"I am a professional nanny," Nanny Nan said with great dignity. "Not a professional . . . kidnapping prevention service. You may consider this my resignation, effective immediately. I will send you an invoice for my services up until today. Good day to you all."

And with that, Nanny Nan marched past the twins, past the Professor, and, with a final glare in her direction, past Cassie. The last everyone saw of her, she was striding down the street.

This, I need not tell you, came as both a shock and, in truth, a pleasant surprise to John and Abigail. They did not want Nanny Nan to be dead, and she wasn't. But they weren't crazy about her continuing to act as their nanny, and now she wasn't that, either. The twins did not go as far as to literally jump up and down and cry, "YAAAY!" but they felt something along those lines. Indeed, John and Abigail exchanged a look that said, wordlessly, "YAAAY!"

The policeman sat down with the Templetons and took their statements. Professor Templeton and John and Abigail told Officer Timmons about Dean D. Dean, his brother, Dan D. Dean, and everything that had happened. The officer said that the police would keep an eye out for the Dean twins.

Then, after Officer Timmons had left and the Professor was taking a little rest, the Templeton twins took Cassie for a walk around the block.

I don't know if you have ever walked a dog before, but if you have, you may have noticed that walking a dog provides a very good opportunity for a calm discussion with someone, even if that someone happens to be the dog. If the someone is another person, all the better. Now that the wild, dangerous adventure with the Dean brothers had come to an end, the Templeton twins were glad to have a chance to talk the whole thing over.

"I bet none of this would have happened if we had stayed at Elysian University," John said.

Abigail nodded. "I still don't understand why we had to leave," she said.

While the twins thought about that, Cassie took the opportunity to spot a squirrel in a tree, grow electrified with excitement, scamper over to the tree, bark, and be dragged away by John.

"Well," Abigail said, "Papa said that the people at Tick-Tock Tech were happy to let him use their laboratory in exchange for teaching."

"I know," John said. "But the people at Elysian University were already doing that. He was using *their* labs and teaching."

Abigail agreed. "He had been doing that since before we were born. Plus, all the students and professors at Elysian University loved him. He knew everybody and everybody knew him. Everybody knew us—and Mama, too."

At the mention of their mother, both twins became silent and slightly sad. It went without saying that, if their mother had still been alive, none of these taxing and frightening events would have happened.

In fact, the thought of staying in this new house, in which so many upsetting things had happened, was not a pleasant one. John said as much, and Abigail agreed. It was only then that the Templeton twins reached a rather intelligent realization.

"Oh," John said.

"Yes," Abigail said. "That explains it."

By then they had returned home. The twins unclipped the leash from Cassie's collar and watched as she sped down the hall to the kitchen and her water bowl, where she lapped and gulped and slurped as though she

had just walked across a desert and not around a perfectly nice, tree-shaded block.

The twins then went to their father's study. The door was open. The Professor was at his desk, jotting notes and humming a little song. They knocked. He looked up. "Papa?" Abigail said. "Can we ask you something?"

Professor Templeton put his pen down and said, "Of course." As the twins entered the study, he added, in a very serious tone, "But first I have to tell you something." The twins sat in the matching chairs their father kept on the other side of his desk and wondered what could cause him to sound so grave. Hadn't the worst possible thing in the world already happened? A year earlier?

"I have neglected to do an important thing," Professor Templeton said. "I have not told you two how very, very proud I am of both of you. What you did was absolutely extraordinary."

"Really?" asked John.

"Really," the Professor replied. "Getting away from that horrible man and that terrible basement . . . finding a way to get him to drive you to where we were in the

woods . . . throwing away those bullets so that nobody could use the gun . . . It was all quite brilliant!"

"That was Abigail's idea," John said.

"And tricking that awful Mr. Dean into hovering where all the Frisbees would be—"

"That was John's idea," Abigail said.

"Absolutely superb. It would have been fantastic had an adult thought of such things. The fact that you two did makes it all the more amazing." He sighed. "I suppose you got some of that ability from me. But you got most of it from your mother. She was always able to . . . to step back from something and see . . . " He gulped and said, with some difficulty, "Well, she could see things that I couldn't."

The twins looked at each other. Finally John said, "That's what we wanted to ask you."

"That's why we had to move, isn't it?" Abigail said.

The Professor looked down at the papers on his desk, swallowed again, and nodded. It was difficult for him to speak.

Then he sighed and sat back. "Yes. There were just too many memories back at the old house. And at Elysian. I suppose that's why I was afraid to go outside until we got Cassie. Then when we went on those nice walks, I decided I could go back to work. But every place I went . . . every person I ran into reminded me of your mother." He smiled at them. "I'm sorry that it upset your lives so much."

"That's all right, Papa," Abigail said. "It's interesting to move to a new place."

"That's very understanding of both of you," the Professor said. "You two are not only lovely children, you are turning into excellent people." The twins could think of nothing to say to this, so they just sat there and felt splendid. Then Professor Templeton cleared his throat and said, "Yes, good. So I may as well tell you now. This entire incident, and what happened to Nanny Nan . . . I . . . I just don't think I can remain in this house. Or at this university. It would be full of unpleasant memories, too."

Abigail said, "You mean—"

"—we're moving again?" her brother said.

Their father nodded. The Templeton twins listened as he explained how he had just come up with a new idea and a new invention, and he had discussed it with people at a new university, and they said they would be delighted if he were to use their laboratories and facilities to develop the new idea and perhaps teach a class or two.

And, indeed, that is what came to pass. But will you be terribly shocked if I suggest that that is another story entirely? And that I have worked quite hard enough in telling you this one? That I deserve a rest, and perhaps a snack, and some sort of recreational fun such as going to the movies or attending a play? Will you be terribly put out if I declare that this, finally, is The End?

Too bad. Because that is exactly the case.

This is, you may be sure,

The

*End.*

## QUESTIONS FOR REVIEW

1. Wasn't this the best book you have ever read?

2. True or false (circle one): This is the best book I have ever read.     T

3. Do you think this is The End?

   a. Really?

## Q&A WITH AUTHOR ELLIS WEINER, ILLUSTRATOR JEREMY HOLMES, AND THE NARRATOR (THE *REAL* TALENT BEHIND *THE TEMPLETON TWINS HAVE AN IDEA*)

ELLIS WEINER

JEREMY HOLMES

THE NARRATOR

### What inspired you to write *The Templeton Twins Have an Idea*?

**Ellis Weiner:** I thought it would be fun to write for a younger audience, who seem up for anything in terms of absurdity. Also, I realized that such an audience would be perfect—

**The Narrator:** Ahem! It may interest you to know that, in fact, the individual who narrates *The Templeton Twins Have an Idea*—and who, therefore, can actually be said to have "created" it—is not Mr. Ellis Weiner. Mr. Weiner is merely a person whose name is on the cover. I will say that I was compelled to narrate *The Templeton Twins Have an Idea* for reasons and by forces I am not disposed to reveal at this time. They may be divulged at a later date.

### What inspired the look of *The Templeton Twins Have an Idea*?

**Jeremy Holmes:** The overall look of the book was inspired by a folded-up set of worn blueprints I found tucked in the back of an old machine parts catalog. There was something about the blurred lines and faded imagery that fit the inventive, yet offbeat mood of the story. As for the illustrations, they drew their inspiration from the unnecessarily complex and humorous gadgety gizmos of W. Heath Robinson, Storm P. (Robert Storm Petersen), and the infamous Rube Goldberg.

### What is your studio like?

**Jeremy Holmes:** Here's a photo of my workspace.

### What was your inspiration for the ridiculous dog?

**Ellis Weiner:** The hyperactive, white, constantly-electrified smooth-haired fox terrier named Cassie in the book is somewhat based on a hyperactive, white, constantly-electrified smooth-haired fox terrier named Cassie, which I used to own. In fact, forget "somewhat." The twins' dog is my (late) dog.

**The Narrator:** Mr. Ellis Weiner insisted that the twins obtain such a dog, and I had no choice but to go along with the whole ridiculous business. I am not, you will be unsurprised to learn, "a dog person."

### What was your favorite thing to do when you were John and Abigail's age?

**Ellis Weiner:** Play softball and touch football, and read. I do play the drums, but I didn't start until I was sixteen.

**The Narrator:** Collect postage stamps from many lands, build scale models of aircraft carriers, and pretend to conduct symphony orchestras being played on the hi-fi.

**Jeremy Holmes:** I'm not one of those people who've always known they were destined to become an artist. As a kid, I had a giant-size appetite for play, which made it impossible for me to sit down for any extended period of time. This would handcuff the development of my artistic abilities until college. After trying my hand at architecture, web design, and graphic design, I finally realized what occupation I could funnel my still sizable appetite for play into: children's books.

## What was your favorite book when you were a child?

**Ellis Weiner:** I didn't have a favorite book so much as favorite series, which were Tom Swift (Jr.), and Tom Corbett, Space Cadet. Or maybe *The Complete Sherlock Holmes*.

**The Narrator:** My favorite book is *The McFundleboom Dictionary of the English Language*—not because I read it, but because I don't have to. I already know that it agrees with me about everything.

**Jeremy Holmes:** My favorite picture book as a child was Bill Peet's *Hubert's Hair-Raising Adventure*. The image of Hubert's mane at the end still makes me chuckle.

## What is your motto?

**Ellis Weiner:** I don't have one. If I did, it would be something like, "Beware people with mottoes."

**Jeremy Holmes:** "Don't be caught without a napkin."

**The Narrator:** Don't be ridiculous! I don't have a motto. I do, however, have a list of FAQs (Frequently Asked Questions, which, as you may know, are questions that are asked frequently).

1. Huh?

2. Are you serious?

3. How come?

4. Wait—what?

5. Really?

6. What time is it?

7. But why?

8. Do we have to?

9. How should I know?

10. What do you mean?

### What profession other than your own would you like to attempt?

**Ellis Weiner:** Theoretical physics.

**The Narrator:** Professional ice dancer.

**Jeremy Holmes:** Dessert chef.

### What's the funniest question anyone has asked you at a book event or school visit?

**Ellis Weiner:** "Do you know that we have an eight-year-old student here whose name is also Ellis Weiner?"

**The Narrator:** "What is it about Ellis Weiner that you admire most?"

### Can you tell us what the Templeton twins will be up to in book two?

**Ellis Weiner:** The Professor will take them to the Thespian Academy of the Performing Arts and Sciences (TAPAS), where he will invent a breakthrough theatrical device and the Dean twins will try to obtain rights to it. There will be a new nanny, the same old (and ridiculous) Cassie, and the twins will get into and out of various scrapes as only they can.

**The Narrator:** Does it matter? So long as I am narrating it?

THE TEMPLETON TWINS

MAKE A SCENE

BOOK 2

WRITTEN BY
ELLIS WEINER

ILLUSTRATED BY
JEREMY HOLMES

O h, no, John!" cried Abigail Templeton to her brother. "Six dancing dinosaurs have kidnapped our dog, Cassie, and taken her to Paris, France!"

"We must thwart them at once, Abby!" replied John. "But first I must have my appendix removed!"[1]

The Templeton twins had been living in their new house for about a week, doing all the things they usually did—going to school and coming home, completing their homework, pursuing their hobbies, caring for Cassie (their ridiculous dog), and making meals—before Saturday finally came, and their father, the famous Professor Elton Templeton, was able to give them a tour of the college where he had recently started working.

So, after a breakfast of waffles and bananas, the twins climbed into the car, along with their (still-ridiculous) dog, and their father drove them to the campus.

Now, if I know you, you are wondering: "What took the Professor so long to show the twins around?" I'll tell you, because you deserve to know. Well, wait. I'm not so

---

1. If you have read the Introductions, you know just how seriously to take this explosive, thrilling, thought-provoking news. If you haven't, then you don't. Let's move on.

sure you do deserve to know. But I will tell you anyway, as a favor. Then you'll owe *me* a favor.[2]

The Professor had been unable to give the twins a tour of the new college right away because it was very important that he get to work immediately. Over the past few years, the college had not had enough students, and so was in danger of going out of business. The college had hired Professor Templeton and given him an urgent, vital assignment: to create an invention that would be so wonderful and remarkable and splendid that colleges and universities all over the world would want to buy one for themselves. Money from those sales would make it possible for the Professor's college to remain in business.

And so, for the first week, the Professor did nothing but attend meetings and think of ideas and work calculations and sketch out basic designs for a new invention.

The name of the college was the Thespian Academy of the Performing Arts and Sciences. People called it TAPAS, for short. Now, I happen to be one of the few

---

2. Please remember this, because it is quite possible I will ask you for a favor later on in this very book.

people who know that the word "tapas" is a Spanish word for a series of appetizerlike snacks served in small portions on small plates at bars and restaurants—very often, in world-famous Spain itself.

In this case, however, the name TAPAS is what we call an "acronym," which is a made-up word formed by the first letters of a chain of words or names. For example, FAQ is an acronym for Frequently Asked Question[3]. Similarly, TAPAS is an acronym for the Thespian Academy of the Performing Arts and Sciences.

Yes, I know: The first letters of "of" and "the" and "and" do not appear in TAPAS. That is often the case: The

---

3. Frequently Asked Questions, as you may know, are questions that are asked frequently. I have my own list of Frequently Asked Questions (FAQs). Here it is:

**The Narrator's FAQs (Frequently Asked Questions)**

1. Huh?
2. Are you serious?
3. How come?
4. Wait—what?
5. Really?
6. What time is it?
7. But why?
8. Do we have to?
9. How should I know?
10. What do you mean?

first letters of unimportant or inessential words often do not appear in acronyms. This is perfectly normal and nothing to be upset about.

This college was devoted to teaching acting, singing, dancing (or "dance," as people who dance refer to dancing), and the many other important crafts and technical skills related to performances of all kinds.

Each building resembled an object or a symbol that was in some way connected with that department's art or craft or skill. For example, the Department of Acting occupied two buildings that were shaped like the famous dual—one might even say "twin"—masks of Comedy and Tragedy that are commonly used to symbolize Drama. The Department of Script Writing was in the form of an immense typewriter. The Department of Wardrobe was shaped like a gigantic armoire.[4] And so on.

"Look at these statues," said Abigail Templeton as she, her brother, their father, and their notably silly dog strolled around campus. "They look kind of . . . tired."

4. "Armoire" is a French word. You pronounce it "arm-WHAH." It means—I think—"a place to keep your arms." Or maybe not. Look, never mind what it means.

It was true. The central quad ("quad" is what colleges insist on calling their big, grassy yards), and many of the spaces between the buildings, were decorated with statues of actors, singers, dancers, directors, playwrights, gaffers, grips, d-girls, and best boys.[5] But all of them were chipped, or rusted, or had pieces missing.

The Professor nodded. He said,

**THIS PLACE IS IN TROUBLE. THAT'S WHY WE'RE HERE.**

---

5. I have no idea what those last four jobs involve. Do you? Oh, please. You do not.